NOT A SIMPLE CRUSH

BY: DEE CROSS

CHAPTER 1

The First Look

We met during the Summer of 2006. I was young and he was young without a clue of what to become. It was his gentle smile that caught my eyes and created a world of wonder. Wondering what life would be like together. Immediate thoughts of how our kids would look and where we would spend the rest of our lives together. Would it be Florida, or would we stay Georgia bound? All the thoughts of the future rushed into my head as I watched him, stalker like. Weird, I know, but at the time it felt right. Especially given the fact that I was 18 years old, practically still a baby and he was 21 years old, damn near grown as hell. Just the way I like them, 3 to 5 years older than me or maybe even a little older than that. He seemed perfect to me. His eyes were perfect brown, his lips full and succulent, his arms built all muscular and thick, he had a low fade haircut lined so perfectly. All I could think to myself is,

Yesssssss. Let me not forget about his teeth, perfectly bright and straight. I was about to start the mission of pursuing him and making him fall so deep in love with me that he wouldn't even dream about another woman.

I walked by him with my curvy body swaying left to right, then right to left. I thought to myself, *This walk is about to put a spell on him*. As I walked past him and his brothers, I could feel his eyes touch my heart. I know, that's deep right. Notice I said touch my heart and not my ass. I knew then the mission had begun. I walked in the house and quickly peeped through the side of the curtain to watch his reaction with his brothers. He seemed to be smiling extra hard now. I knew they were talking about me. It made me feel good. I live only seconds away from him so I can watch his every move. By seconds away I mean I lived right in front of him. Literally across the street. I would have nothing but time to seduce him.

This was my senior year of high school and I thought I had it all figured out. As in where I would be attending college, what type of career I would have, how many kids I wanted, and what type of man I desired to accomplish all of these great things life has to offer. At that moment, the guy across the street looked like he would fit perfectly into my plans. I lived with my mom and sister. My mom met our dad when she was my age. She said that meeting our dad was the best thing that could have happened to her. He made her feel like life could be just like a fairy tale movie. Then he passed away five years ago from a horrible car accident. Just like that my mom's fairy tale movie became a horror movie. My mom had been going to therapy for her grief every day. She was beyond busy with work and therapy sessions and sometimes it felt like that's all she does. She didn't have much time for me and my sister. We had to figure life out the hard way, with most things we ended up teaching ourselves. One of the things I learned very quickly were the gifts I was blessed with in order to catch a man and keep his attention.

I stared into the mirror and I said to myself *Dynver Girl, you're it. You've got perfect feet, beautiful legs, curvy hips, nice size ass, slim waist, smooth abs, perfect boobs (cup size 34B), with a gorgeous face, soft ass lips and seductive eyes. And that's just the outside wait until he sees the inside. Your BIG heart and funny personality just won't stop popping and will surely win him over.* Now all I had to do was get him to speak to me. In the game of love and attention, the person who speaks first loses. Which will mean I had him right where I want him, and he won't even know it. That night I tossed and turned and with every turn I smiled as my mind could not let go of the dreams of how my plan to conquer this human would turn out. Morning came and

I had the perfect plan to get him to speak to me. I waited patiently on my front porch for him to come outside and go for his daily run. Before he started his run, I decided to play the role of damsel in distress. With the hood of my black 1998 Honda Accord raised, I had my sexy ass body posed and leaning over the engine. I was perfectly fitted into a white tank top with booty shorts showing nothing but thighs and skin. I could feel him staring. Then I felt him jogging over, thinking, “Oh my God he’s here. He Has fallen for it. Here goes nothing.”

CHAPTER 2

SPEAK IT INTO

EXISTENCE

"Hey" he said. I looked up with a stressed-out look on my face and with annoyance of his presence displayed and said, "Hey". "What happened to your car? Do you need help?" He said to me while standing in front of me with every defined muscle in his arm and chest calling out for me. I then said to him, "Yes, I guess I could use a hand. But I must warn you I don't know what's wrong with it and I don't know much about cars so don't ask me any questions." I gave a little laugh at the end, knowing men like a little corniness even if they act like they don't. He then leaned over and took a look around. I knew about a week ago it was time for an oil change because the little light on the dashboard had given me a warning maybe a month ago. Lucky for me he checked the oil and what do you know? There's no oil in there. He turned and smiled at me when he said, "Well, it looks like you don't have any oil in your car." "Really?", I replied with a suspenseful look on my face. "Yeah, it's an easy fix you just need to get an oil change or I can take you to the store and show you what kind of oil you need for your car". "Aww thank you, that's so sweet but I don't want to take up too much more of your time." I said this while predicting his next words as he said them: "You're not taking up any of my time". "Are you sure?", I asked. He replied exactly how I hoped, "Yes I'm sure".

The ride to the store was quiet as if he had lost words and didn't know how to steer a conversation. I positioned myself in the seat, crossing my legs over one another and placing my hands in my lap, making sure he can see the dimple in my beautiful brown skinned thighs. I realized that we had not been properly introduced yet and that means I'm technically riding in the car with a total stranger. I knew his name from hearing it around, and I'm pretty sure he knew my name due to the town being super small, but I wanted him to tell me his name. With a soft-spoken voice, I said to him, "So, Stranger, are you not going to tell me your name?" He looked at me with a smile and said, "Sure Stranger, my name is KC and I'm pretty sure you knew that already." I replied, "Well, yes, I know your name but I don't think we are officially not strangers until we properly introduce ourselves." He agreed with a nod then said, "So you're not going to tell me your name? Formally, that is?" I looked at him with a glare in my eyes and I said, "My name is Dynver."

"So Mr. KC, how much longer before we arrive at the store?" I asked. "We're here." I looked up and the ride wasn't so long after all.

We left the store with the oil I needed. On the ride back he asked me the magical question that any person wants to know, "So Ms. Dynver are you seeing anyone?" I looked up and out the car window because at this moment you need to seem shy about answering this question and I finally said, "Not at the moment." The car was silent for all of 20 seconds and I thought to myself how awkward this was. Maybe he was leaving me time to ask him in return. I knew to never be the one to ask if they were seeing someone, not even after they had asked me. You want to have a level of confidence that shows you don't care if he was seeing someone, because you know you're going to seduce him to where he will end it all just to be with you. Plus, that would be admitting that you're interested, and you don't want that just yet. So, play hard to get. I knew the next step was to ask "Why did you ask me that?" The typical answer would be: "It was just a question." Urgh. I hate it when guys don't know how to explain or be honest in any type of way. I suppose I would have to train him in this area.

We arrived just as quickly back to my house. I exited the car and told him thank you for the ride. He smiled and said, “You’re welcome.” I totally forgot I was a damsel in distress. I told him I should have it from here. He said, “OK” and then drove his car into his driveway. I watched him park his 2002 Blue Chevy Caprice and walk into his house. I said to myself, out loud, “I’m going to get you and make you mine”. I didn’t know my meddling sister was listening nearby. “I knew you had a thing for him,” she said as I stood there in a daze. I finally snapped out of it and said, “Kimber is there something I can help you with?” She laughed and said, “No, I’m just observing.” She walked back to the door and looked at me and said, “Speak it into Existence Girl!” I smiled knowing that’s exactly what I was doing.

CHAPTER 3

HE STILL HASN'T ASKED FOR MY NUMBER

It had been two whole days since the car ride to the store and since then he had only smiled my way. He made no attempt at any small talk or to ask for my number. What was the problem? Was I too young to have him be interested in me? Was he afraid people would find out and judge because of our age differences? What was his freaking deal?

Ok, so while I waited patiently on KC to spark the conversation and ask for my number, I decided to resume attention from some of the other male species. There was this one guy named Maxwell who was very interested in me. He was what many would call the Kappa type. You know, the super clean pretty boy type. He had a full black beard, and oh how I loved a man with a nice, thick, clean-cut beard. His bottom lip was perfectly pink and juicy. His eyes told a story of pure romance.

The waves of his hair were perfectly groomed. Yeah, he was a cutie. Although he seemed like he would be the perfect guy to give my attention to, I was just not that into him. I kept him close enough to where he would continue to pursue me until I figured out more about KC.

I invited Maxwell over to my house just to visit and share some laughs. When we were together, we had a great time. It was almost like child play. Maxwell was only a year older than me and maybe that was why I enjoyed his company so much. We had much more in common age wise. He seemed so into me and said and does all the right things. His spiritual connection was aimed in the right direction. I guess I was not that into him because he seemed too good to be true. Although I know I had the looks inside and out, it feels like I would have to fight all my life to keep his attention focused on me because all the girls our age wanted him. Girls were always throwing themselves at him. I told him once that we could never be together because he had too many girls chasing him. Of course, he said the sweetest thing ever back in response. He said to me, “Yeah all these girls are chasing me but I’m chasing you.” You see what I mean? Either he was too perfect or I’m too afraid to trust him, or both.

While me and Maxwell sat outside on my front porch, KC parked his car in his driveway across the street. I slid a little closer to Maxwell to create a look of intimacy for KC but not so much to leave a gray area of friends only vibe for Maxwell. I noticed KC glance over at us. He didn't smile or give any inkling that he was remotely concerned that another male had my attention. Yet, he didn't seem happy about it either. Maxwell was sitting next to me with a big ass smile on his face as if I were finally letting him get close. When KC walked into the house, I smoothly slid myself back away from Maxwell and suggested that we go hangout at the SPOT. The SPOT was a place where underaged people ages 18-20 could vibe and listen to music, like a bar but with no alcohol involved. I loved the SPOT because I loved to dance, and Mr. Perfect Maxwell loves to dance as well.

We arrived at The SPOT and Maxwell held my hand as we walked. Such a perfect gentleman, I know. I smiled the entire time I was with him, but I couldn't get my mind off of KC. We were not a couple nor were we exes, yet I kept wondering, *Was he upset to see me with another man? Does he believe he missed his opportunity? Am I just overthinking the entire thing?* I danced and danced and danced all night with Maxwell. All the other girls that wanted him were staring at me with hate in their eyes. I didn't like this type of attention. Which would be another reason why I liked my guys older, none of the girls my age would be concerned. They were too busy being worried about HIGH SCHOOL love. I was looking for some real grown, build together, type of love. You could only find that in older men.

While me and Maxwell were dancing our asses off, here came this big breasted, big booty girl he used to date. Her name was Shantel and rumor is every time Maxwell tried to move on and date someone new she interfered and bullied the new girl in his life with lies and harassment. Anything to keep the new girl from moving forward with him. I did not understand girls my age. Why is it she had to be concerned with who he was dating? Why couldn't she just move on? She was not a rough looking girl. She was actually really nice looking. Shantel was a redbone with long black hair, big breasts, big booty, thin waist, thick thighs and hazel eyes. Her skin tone alone could get her any man she wanted – colorism - but no, she wanted MAXWELL and Maxwell only. She walked near us on the dance floor and stood there with her two best friends. I could feel him getting uncomfortable, so I did what I do best, I put on a show. I grinded my ass into his pelvic seductively. Then I turned around and grabbed his hands and placed them around my waist as I pulled myself close to him, slowly winding up and down. Making sure she knew I would not be intimidated as easily as the other girls. He enjoyed every second of it. I could tell she wasn't pleased, but if she only knew I'm not all that interested in him. On the ride home we conversed about the awkwardness Shantel displayed for him. Actually, he mostly did all the talking while I sat there wondering what my next move would be to seduce KC. We arrived in my driveway and Maxwell had this look on his face like he would like to ask me for a kiss. I told him I had a good time tonight and would see him later. When I exited the car, I decided to give him a little peck on the cheek just to keep him around a little bit longer.

Maxwell drove off and as I turned to walk up to my door I heard a voice from a distance say, "Hey Dynver." I turned around and it was him. KC. I said hey back with a friendly smile. He started jogging towards me, and I stood there secretly excited that he was coming over. He approached me and said "Wassup?" I thought to myself, *Really dude? How about you say something like Prince Charming would say, like I'm here Princess Dynver. Ready for you to be my Queen…you know some fairy tale bullshit. Not this wassup shawty shit.* Instead, I responded all shy like, "Nothing. What's up with you?" He licked his lips all LL Cool J style and said, "Nothing just chilling outside, I could really use some company if you don't mind joining me." Here it was, he had initiated conversation. I said ok and we walked back to his yard. It was night out and the moon was shining bright. The air was warm and with every step, this felt like heaven. We sat and chatted about nothing really and I wasn't surprised. KC was not really much of a conversationalist like Maxwell, but he didn't have to say much because I enjoyed him watching me. He spoke very briefly and kept it at basic and simple questions. He asked questions such as where do you work? What kind of music do you like? Oh, and what do you like to do? You know, quick Q&A's. I believe I answered everything pretty simply. I could've made the conversation more interesting, but I honestly just was still in shock that he had even approached me. We sat for a few minutes in total silence. Awkward yet enjoyable, just being with him raised my hormones. He then said, "Well it's getting late and I have to go to work in the morning, so I will walk you home." I turned and said to him, "OK, and I live right across the street so there's no need for you to walk me home. You can just watch me." I meant that with every bit of me, all I wanted him to do was watch me. If I knew nothing else about myself, I knew I had a mean strut when I walked and that I could take a man's soul with my eyes. I started walking back to my house and I looked back once I reached the door and saw KC was still watching. I waved my hand and he nodded his head. I took a shower and laid down in my comfy queen-sized bed and then it dawned on me. HE STILL DIDN'T GET MY NUMBER.

CHAPTER 4

SAME STRAW

It had been almost an entire week and he had yet to initiate conversation again or ask me for my number. He would speak when he saw me, but that's it. Just hearing his deep voice say my name with so much passion tickled my spine a little bit every time. It was time for plan B: Include myself in his circle. I decided to make friends with some of his close friends and relatives. This should have been easy for me, due to the fact that I already attended high school with a male cousin of his. There was no reason for any alarm or intrigue about it being a male cousin. He was not into girls like me if you catch my drift. I entered the lunchroom at school and there he was, Derrick, the coolest LGBT person I had met yet. I walked up to him and started making small talk. He invited me to a kick back they were having at a nearby relative's house. I accepted the invite knowing exactly why it was a must that I be there. Derrick agreed to pick me up. He had no idea that he's playing the role of a wingman.

Derrick reached my house by 8:30 PM. His music was banging incredibly loud and the choice of song was my type of ratchet, Ludacris feat Pharrell – "Money Maker". Well, here goes nothing. I knew KC had already left to attend the party because I'd watched him, and his brothers get in his car. They were dressed for the occasion and left about 30 minutes ago. Derrick and I arrived at the kick back fashionably late by one hour. And when I say, "fashionably", I mean me and Derrick were both looking good. Derrick had on his blue jeans with a clean crease, with his cowboy belt buckle, white Nike air forces that were super clean, and a button-up striped shirt. To top it all off, he had diamonds in both of his ears. I exited the vehicle with my new red sandals that had straps going up my beautiful legs and showed off my perfectly pedicured toes, blue jean shorts cut just below the curve of my ass, and a loose white sheer blouse with a red lace bralette. I knew all eyes were on me. I only cared about and wanted one set of eyes on me though, and at the moment those brown eyes were nowhere to be found. Where in the hell was he? About 45 minutes flew by and although I was having a good time, I still had not seen a glimpse of Mr. K.C. yet. I started to wonder if he had attended another party. The house was not that big, so I was certain I didn't miss him.

The party started to get more crowded and as I looked at the entrance door, there he was. My eyes brightened with relief that he had finally made it to the party. I quickly stood near the hunch punch bowl where I could be easily noticed. When he looked my way, our eyes met, and I could feel the sparks through that invisible connection. He walked up to me and said, "Hey, what are you doing here?" I smiled and spoke with a friendly voice over the loud music, "Hanging out with a classmate. His name is Derrick." He seemed surprised and said, "Oh yeah, that's my cousin. I didn't know you knew each other." I nodded my head in agreement. Derrick and some of his home girls came over and grabbed me by the hand to dance with them. When I stepped onto the living room floor I started to dance, but the entire time my eyes were locked on KC. With every rock of my hips and vibration of my ass I made sure to stare at him. As the night got darker and people slowly started to go home, Derrick was still crunk and clearly drunk. I asked Derrick what time he would be able to take me home. Derrick looked at me with the one eye he had open and his posture slumped and said, “Bitch, I’m too drunk to take you home.” KC overheard the conversation and said to me with his deep stern voice, “I’ll take you home, STRANGER”. I looked at him and replied “Thanks, Stranger.”

On the way home my stomach did the unthinkable. It growled and it wasn’t like we were talking or anything to where the growl could’ve been mistaken for anything other than what it clearly was. I looked at him and he looked at me and of course he asked, “Are you hungry?” I mean I was, but I was already in need of a ride home and asking him to take me to get something to eat seemed like a bit too much. Before I could reply he said, “I’m hungry myself. If it's ok with you, maybe we can go grab a bite to eat at the Waffle House?” *Well*, I thought to myself, *I don’t see anything wrong with getting some grub, especially since I haven't really eaten today, and I never eat at other people's houses*. "Sure" I responded.

We sat at a table and ordered our food. I sat there all nervous because this definitely was not a part of my plan yet. We started chatting and the conversation was pretty much filled with laughter. No real serious questions were asked, just jokes and laughs about others at Waffle House and people from the party. He was laughing at my jokes and they sounded like real laughs, not the type of fake or forced laughs where it's like yeah let me laugh at your joke but you're not all that funny. He really thought I was funny. That was a good thing. The waitress brought us our food and we eat. I ordered a Fanta orange soda to go with my meal. I don't know why because I never really finish soda. When we were leaving, I asked for a to-go cup. I didn't want it to seem like I wasted his money on the soda since he paid. We were riding down the street and I took two sips out of the drink from my straw. He looked over and said, "That drink looks good. Do you mind if I have a sip?" I replied by handing him my drink and he placed his lips on my straw and took 3 big gulps. He then gave me back the drink. Now even if I wanted to, I couldn't drink my drink again. Thoughts started rushing through my head. *Why did he do that? Does he trust that I don't have any STDS? What made him think I want his lips on my straw?* As we got closer to our street I noticed a park nearby, and without asking he drove his car into the parking lot. I sat there quietly not asking any questions. As he put the car in park, I finally came to and asked, "Why are we here?" He looked at me and said, "Your sister told me that you may have a crush on me". As I sat there looking crazy as hell the first thought that rushes through my head is, *Why the hell would she do that?* He continues, "Honestly I think I have a crush on you. I've noticed you since you moved across from us. The way you walk, smile, and talk just really catches my attention." I could not believe he was saying all of this. I looked at him and said, "I can't believe my sister told you that. I'm going to kill her." I gave KC a desirable stare, I looked into his eyes and tried to reach to his soul and then said, "I think you're cute and interesting. I've noticed you as well and I would definitely like to get to know you better." He leaned in and said, "OK, so can I have your number?" I gave him my digits and I looked down at my Fanta orange soda drink and took two sips out of my straw.

CHAPTER 5

NO ONE KNOWS

KC called me almost every night. Although each conversation was only about 3 minutes long when we spoke over the phone, in person we were having some serious body conversations. We made out every night. It always started with him first caressing my body and then dipping me into his arms while he held my head for support, then he would kiss me from my lips to my neck and then back again. Kissing is one of my favorite things to do. I would kiss all night if he would let me. We made out every night and everywhere. There were times when we made out at his job while he was on lunch or on a quick break. We made out in his house, my house, in his car, in my car, in the garage and in the park. I enjoyed every minute of it and there was not a question in my head if he was enjoying it too. I knew he couldn't get enough of me.

Graduation was approaching sooner rather than later for me and I had plans to attend college at Florida State University. Although that was the plan, I had yet to receive the acceptance letter. I was still patiently waiting. I had prayed and prayed about it and I know I had the good grades and can go anywhere but Florida is where I wanted to be (#beachlife). I loved the ocean and to be anywhere near it was a huge plus. KC and I never really talked much about college and my future life goals. Did he even care? And why hadn't I made it a point to mention my goals to him? And what were his long-term goals? Was him working his 9-5 his only goal? All these questions rushed to my brain. Had I just been overwhelmed with lust that I failed to get to know the real him? Or better yet, had I neglected to have him reap the benefits of knowing the intelligent individual I am?

I met up with KC while he was at work. It was raining out and the rain was always the perfect time for us to make out in the car. Just to hear the sound of the rain thumping on the roof of the car while his hands were all over me was giving me chills and excitement. The slow strokes that deepened into me with every stroke sent me to another place of total relaxation and enjoyment as I moaned. When every inch of him entered me I whispered to him in his ear, "I love you". Why had I just said that? Did I know what love was? Was he going to say it back? Did he love me? He didn't say it back. Although normally that would drive me crazy, I was glad he didn't, because I wasn't really sure how I felt.

The rain stopped and we were gathering our clothes and putting them back on our sweaty bodies. I was thinking in my head, *he's going to mention those words I used: I love you.* He slid his shoes on and turned towards me, gave me a kiss on my forehead and then said, "OK, text me later, I have to get back to work." I exited the car and weighed down with disappointment. So he really didn't think anything of the words I used. Sure, I was glad he didn't say it back, but it could have at least been a conversation. This was a total turn off for me. I was not sure what I had gotten myself involved with.

On my way home, I began to think about me and KC and what type of relationship we had. I was really focusing on trying to remember all the pros of being with him and how he made me feel. If you hadn't guessed it by now, I was a think-think type of girl. My brain was constantly filled with thoughts. I then questioned myself about why I said those words to him? Was it just in the heat of the moment? Was it really how I feel? If so, then why did I feel this way? I drove my car into the driveway, and I sat there, puzzled. Then I questioned myself. Why hadn't I met his mother or been properly introduced to his brothers? Why is it we only meet at night? I mean sure, during the morning he's resting before he has to go into work and I was attending school. In the evening he was with his friends and I was with mine. On the weekends he was not working, and I didn't have school, yet we still met at night. What was I missing? Then it hit me like a big slap in the face. No one knew about us. I was just his late-night hook up. All I was to him is a fuck. How did this happen?

CHAPTER 6

THE TALK

I've always been a very honest person. Have always able to tell people exactly how I feel. I got that from my mother. She always told me to say what I mean and mean what I say. Which to sum it all up pretty much meant, stand behind everything you say and stand your ground. That is what I needed to do. I needed to have a talk with KC about the other night and how it made me feel. He needed to know that I need more from him and that this fling would not flourish without him making an effort to be more than just a sex buddy. I can't lie, I was a little bit nervous about having this conversation. My body still yearned for his attention and I didn't want to say anything to make him end things with me. Yet I was still certain that I wanted to have the talk. Like a wise person once said, you never know until you ask.

Typically, I would have texted him when I was on the way to meet up with him at his job. Tonight, I decided to not show up at all. That's right, no text, no call, and no show. Of course, I was bored out of my mind because our little late-night flings had become routine for me. He sent a text that read: *Hey, where are you?* I text back: *Hey I'm home*. At this moment, I had decided to reply with a dry response and if he was into me he should notice something was wrong and figure it out. He replied by texting: *Ok, so I guess you don't want to play tonight*. Really?

Is this all he had to say? I gave him my time and energy and he saw fit to consider it to be JUST PLAY. I replied: *No not tonight and plus there is actually something I would like to talk to you about.* I knew just as well as everybody else, no one likes to hear those words, WE NEED TO TALK. He texted back: *Ok*. Why was I so upset with his response? I knew why. It's because I needed him to communicate like a 21 year old instead of a 7 year old.

The next day came and he hadn't sent a text or called all day. Night fell and still no response from him. Not even a where are you text. I became worried that maybe he had just decided to forget me and had already moved on to the next one. Three days passed. I did not reach out to him and he still has not reached out to me. Was he trying to punish me for not showing up that night? I thought to myself, *welp Dynver you blew it*. How could he give me all that passionate love and just disappear like this? I hadn't seen him in days, not even while peeking through the curtains of my bedroom. Where in the hell was he? As I lay there in my bed staring up at the ceiling. I received a text. Before looking to see who it was I said to myself, *it's about time. I don't know if I could've gone another day attempting to give him the silent treatment*. I looked at the phone while smiling from ear to ear. Urgh, it was Maxwell. Why? Why? Why? His text said: *Hey Dynver, I haven't heard from you in a while, what have you been up to?* I roll my eyes because this is the text I've been waiting for just from the wrong man. I was so over it at that moment, I didn't have the energy to reply to Maxwell. I rolled over and forced myself to go to sleep.

It was 2:00 am in the morning and my phone was vibrating. I flipped my phone over to my face to see who could be calling me this late. It was him, KC. I quickly answered the phone while trying to hide the excitement in my voice. I answered with, "Hello." He responded, "How have you been, Stranger?" The nerve of him to ask me how I have been when he's been MIA and just totally dodged me, so I could miss him and forget that we need to talk. I would not fall for it. I responded with, "I've been better". Yeah, that's right. The excitement has left the room. Time to get serious. He then replied with, "Oh yeah, how so?" I was happy I finally had an open question where I could release all the words in the world to explain what I was thinking and how I felt and where the hell has he been and why I haven't heard from him. Yes, it was time to let him have it. While sitting up in my bed with a strong determined look on my face, ready to tell his ass off, I replied, "KC, look, I don't know If you notice or not but I really like you. Like all this time spent with you has been great but I want more from you. Sometimes it seems as If I'm the only one talking about the future and my dreams when we do spend very little time chatting before taking off our clothes. I noticed the other night, before I decided that we needed to talk, that I don't really know much about you and if we're even compatible or if you see me as more than just a booty call. I haven't been introduced to your family nor have I been formally introduced to any of your close friends. No one knows who I am to you. And I don't know how you feel in return. I don't want to seem so serious, but I do want to be more than the girl you call only in the heat of the night." There, I had said it. I hoped I had remembered to say everything that needed to be said. I was hoping it wasn't too much to take in at one time, but I had been holding in these thoughts for days now and the perfect time to explode was then and in that moment. The phone was very quiet and then he said, "Well, I guess this is goodbye." What the hell had just happened here? What did he mean goodbye? Was he serious right now? All those passionate nights and this is what I got. Not even a proper 'I'm sorry', and along with that an explanation. I was sure I deserved an explanation. Oh, he was quite the conversationalist, wasn't he? As we sat on the phone with awkward silence for all of 10 seconds I responded with, "Ok" and then I pressed the end button on my phone. He was so not worth it, I told myself. What had I been thinking? One word can only describe what we had - LUST.

CHAPTER 7

HE WANTS ME BACK

I must admit, I resumed life for myself fairly quickly and with no tears involved. I was sure I had not been in love at all. Most people who are in love and then have to go through a breakup cry, they can't eat, they can't sleep, and they either gain a lot of weight or lose a lot of weight. I did none of it, I stayed my perfect weight and continued to focus on school. I had seen KC since, but he didn't smile my way anymore. There is oddly still something about him that made me want to seek his attention, but I didn't feed into it.

I still haven't received my acceptance letter for FSU. I guess I needed to start considering other options. While I was sitting on my porch, I noticed the mailman place the mail in our mailbox. As I walked to check the mail, KC's car pulled into his driveway.I stood there so that he could see what he's missing while I was looking through the mail. Still no letter from FSU. I looked up to see If I could catch a glimpse of him watching me, instead I froze as I saw another female walking next to him. I immediately thought to myself, *what the hell KC? It's only been one week since our little goodbye and you've already moved on.* I watched him as he opened the door for her, and they walked into his house. Who the hell was she?

I sat on the porch waiting on them to finally leave. I would sit here all day just to get a closer look at her. To see what it was she had that I didn't. Why did she get to meet the family? How long had they actually been talking? It could not have been that long because I had been seeing him for 6 months and we only been done with each other for a week. Could he have been seeing her the entire time he was sleeping around with me? Was I the side piece?

I was sitting on my porch desperately waiting for her time to be up. They had been in his house for over three hours now. What were they doing? Was he giving her all the passion he used to give me? Not for 3 hours he wasn't. Finally, they walked out the house and she was smiling and looking very pleased. KC was smiling and held her waist as they walked towards his car. He opened the passenger side door for her and then walked back to the driver side of the car and then he looked directly in my face. I quickly shied away from having eye contact with him. The nerve of him to even look my way.

Later that night Kimber and I decided to have movie night. She loved watching horror movies but me, not so much. I agreed to watch horror movies with her anyway, just to get my mind off KC and his little chicken head looking girlfriend. The movie she selected to watch was SAW IV. Why must she traumatize me right now? We began the movie and I was already feeling a bit nauseous. It was about 45 minutes into the movie and I gave up. Kimber asked where I was going and I replied,

"Girl, you can have this scary shit!" She laughed and continued to watch the movie. I went to go sit on the porch and I noticed KC is not back home yet. I saw a set of car headlights driving down the road and the loud music sounding off lyrics, "Soon as I see her walk up in the club (I'm a flirt) Winkin eyes at me, when I roll up on them dubs (I'm a flirt) Sometimes when I'm with my chick on the low (I'm a flirt)" Yeah, he was happy with himself, clearly I could see this with my own two eyes.

He parked his car and looked over my way. He couldn't possibly have anything to say to me. When he was looking over at me, I foolishly looked back. Then he opened his mouth and said, "Hey Dynver, can we talk?" Was he serious right now? Every bit of me wanted to tell him No! Talk to your new HOE. I chose not to respond with words but gracefully stood up and walked across the street. He didn't move to meet me halfway, he let me walk all the way to his feet. Once I was face-to-face with him, I leaned against his car and said, "Hey". He looked at me and smiled and just like normal he started to make small talk. Always starting with how have you been or what are you up to. I answered his simple questions and the unexpected happened. He said to me, "I know you're upset with the way things ended between us and I want you to know that I never meant to hurt you. I already have a girlfriend and the entire time I was sleeping around with you I was still with her." *Just twist the knife while you already have it in my heart why don't you*, I think to myself. He continued, "You were something fun at the time and I did not notice my wrongdoing until I saw how serious you felt about us." My dumb ass was still standing here listening to his every word. *Move feet move*. "I just want you to know that when I was with you I didn't have much to say because I just admired your beauty and the way you made me feel when we were together. Our bodies pressed against one another was so warm and relieving. I was lost for words and I've never met a girl, I mean a woman, like you that could make me feel the way you did and without me having to try so hard." So he thought I was easy? And just when I thought he had more to say, here it was again, just like old times: the awkward silence. He waited on me to reply but I didn't have any words for him. He finally asked me if I was okay. I nodded my head yes. I was standing there looking pitiful because things didn't turn out the way I had planned for them too. He then asked, “Can we still be friends?” Just like the idiot I was, my heart said NO but my body was screaming Yes! I looked at him and I said, “Sure, friends only, friends without benefits.” He smiled and shook my hand like we're just the best of buds and agreed with a nod.

I walked across the street but not with the same energy I had before. There was no strut in my walk. This was the walk of shame. I cannot believe I agreed to remain friendly with Mr. Disrespectful. He pretty much had just told me to my face that I was his side piece and he wanted his cake and to eat it too. I entered the house. Kimber was standing there with a curious look on her face. She asked me, “Dynver, what's going on with you and KC?” I easily replied while continuing to walk to my room, “Nothing, we’re just friends.” Kimber knew something was off with me, but she would not pry. She is the type who allows me to come to her with my issues on my own time and I like it that way.

I collapsed on my bed, face first. I stuffed my face into my pillow to have a moment of complete silence. My phone started to ring, ring, and ring. I picked it up to look and it was KC calling. Lord, what could he possibly want with me now? I answered the phone and before I could say hello he said, "Come outside" and then he hangs up. I'm so confused right now. I walked out the door and his car was parked in my driveway. I walked up to the driver side of the car and he told me to get in. Following his every command, I got in the car and he drove off. *Where are we going?* I thought to myself. He was quiet, you know, his normal shit. I sat there quietly as well, just trying to see if I could figure out what's actually going to happen. We arrived at the park, which brought back memories. This was where we first talked and where we would sometimes meet to be bodily connected with one another, if you know what I mean. I'm sure that he couldn't possibly think after the talk we just had that I would be willing to give him any more of this good stuff.

He parked the car and we sat there for a while. Neither of us were talking and at this point I didn't know if either of us really knew what to say. Why had he brought me here? Was it to remind me of the intense, passionate love making we used to do here? Was it to confess his real love for me? All I knew was someone better get to talking. I started to remember all the nights we spent in the park. While we sat in his car and with him being only inches away from my body, which is now in heat because my hormones have a mind of their own. I said his name, "KC!", he looked at me and started to lean in. *Oh no, don't do it. Don't you dare try to kiss me. I will not be your sex slave anymore. I do not want any parts of you.* I was lying to myself. As his lips reached mine I told myself to slap him, but my hands didn't listen to the orders my brain was giving. His lips gently kissed mine and what did I do? I kissed him back. Oh Lord, why? The kissing continued and then he took a break from all the kissing and looked me straight in my eyes and said to me, "I want you. I want you all to myself." The kissing continued and we made hot steamy love in his car. I had forgiven him without a second thought.

CHAPTER 8

YOUNG AND DUMB

I woke up with the biggest smile on my face. Last night was the best make-up sex I had ever had. I felt so filled with butterflies and shit. I was singing love songs all morning. Today would be a good day. My face glowed brightly as I danced through the house. I gathered my things and got ready for school. Nothing could tarnish this vibe today. As I walked out the front door, I looked over at KC's house and his car was not in front of his yard. Where was he? Was he with her?

I arrived at school, unable to focus on my class assignments. All I was thinking about was KC. I knew his schedule like the back of my hand. When he dropped me off at my house last night, I watched him pull into his driveway. I was sitting in class with a dazed look on my face. My brain was creating a thousand scenarios of where the hell he could be. Everything in me was telling me he was with her. I thought about all the times he was MIA. He had to have been with her. I no longer wanted to be in school today. I felt sick, so sick to my stomach that I thought I was about to vomit. I stood up to get my teachers attention to let her know that I was not feeling well and needed to see the nurse. Then... *Blaaaaaaaaagh*, I vomited all over the floor.

When I was sitting in the nurse's office, all I could think about was KC. Why was he in my mind so strong? Was it because I know that I made myself look like a gullible little girl and how I wish I had not fallen so easily for him, all over again? The nurse entered the room and she said, "Ms Dynver, what's wrong?" I responded to her while holding my stomach with my back slumped over, "I don't know Mrs. Samuels. I was in class and I felt nauseous and before I could tell Mrs. Patterson, I puked all over the floor." Mrs. Samuels looked at me with a concerned, yet disapproving look on her face and said to me, "Dynver, you can be honest with me here, are you pregnant?" I looked at Mrs. Samuels and I said to her, "WHAT? No Mrs. Samuels. I use protection every time." I lied to her. KC and I never used protection, not even the first time. Mrs. Samuels stared at me with the detective eye every older woman has, you know the stare that says: 'Little girl I've been young before, who do you think you're fooling?'.

Mrs. Samuels asked me if I felt well enough to return to class. I told her no because I desperately needed some time to myself. I had to figure out what the hell KC is up to and I knew I couldn't focus in class knowing he's up to no good. Mrs. Samuels gave me a slip requesting that I go home for the day and report to a doctor within the next 24 hours. On my way home I started thinking about the question Mrs. Samuels asked. Was I pregnant? Not saying that it couldn't happen to me, I mean I had been having sex, but I had other plans. A baby at that very moment would not be a good thing. Now I was desperately curious, could I really be pregnant?

I arrived home and KC's car still was not in his driveway. I had other things to think about right now. I could actually be pregnant. I needed to make a doctor's appointment to show proof to Mrs. Samuels I did as she requested. I called the doctors' office and made my appointment for the next morning. I texted KC saying: *Hey, we need to talk.* Just like the last time, he didn't reply. Urgh, why was he doing this to me? It was 9:00 PM at night and he still had not replied to my text. I was not the type to harass people with thousands of text messages, but I was getting anxious. As I began typing a long text message starting with: *Why the hell haven't you replied to my text message yet and where have you been*? I heard his car pull up in his driveway. I quickly erased the message, making sure not to hit the send button and ran to the front door. I looked across the street and I saw KC, and then I saw her again. The same girl from last time. He didn't waste any time. He shoved it in my face once again, I'm just a hookup. My eyes filled with anger as I stared at them while he was holding her hand, smiling and rubbing the hands that he touched me with all over her. I was disgusted with him but mostly with myself. How did I let myself become the Night Whore?

After, I stood there watching them until they walked in the house. I went to my room and shut my door just to scream in my pillow. *I hate him, I hate him, I hate him*, I repeatedly chanted to myself. Kimber heard me through the thin walls and I guess she couldn't take it anymore. Kimber burst into my room and with a demanding tone she said, "I've sat back long enough waiting on you to share with me what's really going on with you lately, you're going to talk to me, and you're going to talk to me right now!" In desperate need of someone to talk to, I spilled all the beans. Kimber is only one year younger than me, so I didn't expect her to have any answers. We were both young, plus dumb, when it came to relationships and life. She looked at me with shock on her face and said, "Dynver, everything is going to be ok. You are very beautiful and did not deserve to be someone's stress relief. You are young and intelligent with nothing but an excellent future to look forward to. Soon you will be off to college and will meet more interesting guys than KC. You know what momma always says, when you know better, you do better. You can and will do much better than KC. So don't beat yourself up, pick yourself up, and get back to the fun girl that I've missed so much." The pep talk with Kimber really helped. I must admit, I didn't think she could be so encouraging. She made me feel like it's kind of ok to be young and dumb and make some mistakes now. I promised I would be grown instead of foolish moving forward.

I arrived at the doctors' office all by myself. Kimber wanted to come with me, but I assured her I would be fine. I was super nervous. Although I believed I was done with KC, there was a chance I could be pregnant with his baby. The doctor entered the room and we talked about my sexual life, I chose to tell her everything. She knew all the things my young body has experienced, shame on me. She suggested that since I've been having unprotected sex that I should take a pregnancy test and also a STD test. I agreed to everything and she left the room to go retrieve the pregnancy test and her tools to open me up and swab. I sat there patiently waiting for her return and my mind started to wander. Why wasn't I more protective of myself? First, I could possibly be pregnant. Second, now I could possibly have a STD. I said a quick prayer while I was waiting: *Lord, If you get me out of this, I promise to never have sex again until marriage.* The doctor returned to the room and said, “Good news is you will know within seconds if you’re pregnant or not but you will have to wait 48 hours for your STD test results to return.” Wow, I thought to myself, 48 whole hours to know If I have a deadly disease. I peed on the stick and just like she said within seconds the results appeared. The doctor looked at me and said, “Dynver…” I bowed my head down staring into my hands, already disappointed in myself. She continued her statement ,“…you’re NOT pregnant”. *Wooh, that's a relief.* She then told me to check my email within 48 hours and I should see my results for STDs. I exited the doctor's office with one relief down and another to go. KC still had not called or texted me. Maybe that last night with him was his final goodbye. Yet, why would he romantically pause as we kissed just to tell me he wants me and that he wants all of me? I was honestly still confused. I waited on the porch for Kimber to come home so I could fill her in on what the doctor said. While I was waiting, KC arrived, pulling his car into his driveway. Sick of his shit, I quickly went into my house. I did not want to see him at all right now. Yet, I peeped through the curtain to watch his every move. Why must I be so stupid? He got back in his car and left again. I thought to myself, *yeah run off and see your little girlfriend while I sit here patiently awaiting STD results.*

The 48 hours took forever to go past, but today was the day I was supposed to get my results. I checked my email from Doctor Weatherly with my eyes eager to see the words negative, negative, negative. The only sentence it said was for me to visit the office to talk about my results. What the hell did this mean? Oh my God, I was going to DIE. I was too young, why did I make these foolish mistakes? I definitely needed some support on this trip to the doctors. I asked Kimber if she could miss the first and second period of school and come with me to the doctor's office. Just like the sweet nosey little sister she is, of course she agreed. We sat in the room waiting for Dr. Weatherly. Kimber wasn't saying anything and neither was I. I was in deep prayer with the Lord, this had to be a mistake. Dr. Weatherly walked in and said, "Hello Dynver". I needed her to get to it already, to tell me I have an incurable disease and I'm going to DIE. She removed her glasses from her face and said, "You do not have a disease that you cannot get rid of." There was so much relief rushing through my skin, I screamed out "Yessss!" Then she says, "Calm down. You do however have Gonorrhea and we can cure that right now with a shot." With a puzzled look on my face, I turned around and let Dr. Weatherly give me the shot in my ass. The ride home was awkward and I didn't want to talk. Kimber understood I could not attend school after that so she offered to stay home with me but I didn't let her.

I needed to tell KC. He had to know that he was walking around with a deadly weapon in his pants. I knew he would not respond to my text. I texted him anyway. I let him know in the text: *We are done. Don't you ever look my way again. And just so you know. You should probably go get tested for STDs because you gave me Gonorrhea.* I hit the send button and felt relieved that I had finally let go of KC. Still I waited for him to respond. *Bing*, the noise my phone makes when I receive a text message. He texted back, I opened the text message and it read only two letters. This heartless creature replied back with: *OK*. OK? I was upset now. *KC you have done it now. You're about to see what OK looks like.* I stormed down the hall and out the front door, ready to fly across the street to give him a piece of my mind and slash some tires while I was at it. Mid-rage, I was stopped at the mailbox by the mailman. He gave me a package and said to me, "Sorry, this was misplaced with someone else's mail weeks ago." I retrieved the package from the mailman. The package was addressed to me with the FSU stamp. This was it, this was what I had been waiting on. I opened it up with excitement and quickly forgot about KC and his bull. The letter read, "Dear Ms. Dynver Hartage, We are very pleased to accept you as a student at Florida State University". Yes! Yes! Yes! With all the craziness that had been going on this was the best news yet.

CHAPTER 9

GRADUATION

It was graduation day and I was overwhelmed with joy. I knew my mom was proud of me. I thanked God that I had managed to keep all the disappointments out of view. My little secret life of almost being pregnant, possibly with twins because what else could be worse, oh that's right, all while having an incurable disease. Yes, the Lord had given me a second chance. I vowed to myself to never let this happen again. I would protect my heart and my vagina at all costs. As I was putting on my pure white dress that wrapped around my body and showed every delicate curve of me, I got a knock at my bedroom door. I answered the door and it was Kimber. "Work it girl, work it", Kimber said to me as I put on a little catwalk show for her. She had these beautiful red roses in her hands. "Are these for me?" I asked her, knowing they were. She replied with, "Yes, it has your name on it dumb-dumb." "Who are they from?" She was quiet. I looked at her with suspense in my eyes and asked her again, this time with a firmer tone, "Kimber, who are they from?" She looked at me and said his name, "KC". "Kimber, why did you bring me these? You could've just gotten rid of them. Better yet, cursed him out and gotten rid of him." I forgave Kimber, she had not been thinking how this would affect me. She had no clue that I was still working on moving forward. I had not seen KC in a month now. Well, I had seen him, but not like that. I just glanced at him through my curtains from time to time. I saw it as a way to remember the ugly person he was on the inside. I know, it made no sense.

We were getting ready to leave the house when I looked across the street to catch KC staring at me. He and his brother were hanging out in his yard. I told Kimber to go get me the roses out of the trash in the house. She returned with the roses. I stepped down each step with my silver pumps and strutted my way to the outside trash can. My hips moved left to right and right to left with each step being my baddest step ever. I looked over at KC and I stared from the distance right into his eyes as I slammed the roses in the trash. *Yes, Dynver show him he ain't shit and you don't need his gifts*. I had this pep talk to reassure myself that it was over. I knew it shouldn't take all this reassuring, but I needed it. Lately my hormones had been screaming for some male attention, but I was sticking to my word. I would not be participating in any sexual acts until I was married.

I sat there in my chair on the high school football field waiting on my name to be called. I thought of all the exciting things that would happen to me in my future. College was about to be lit. The beach was nearby and whenever I needed a break, I could go and wouldn't have to travel far. I could sit at the beach all day and listen to the waves rushing up to the land, watching it wash my feet free of the sand that I had dug them in. I couldn't wait to be free. Principal Arnold announced my name on the mic: "Dynver Irene Hartage". I walked onto the stage feeling like a star and received my high school diploma. I broke down in tears as I stood there with all my classmates, knowing that I was not the only one who had made mistakes in life. I was just very happy my mistakes didn't cost me my diploma.

After they received their diplomas, all the graduates and guests met in the gym for a graduation party the school had planned. I saw a group of friends that I had not spoken to in a while since this whole KC thing happened. I walked over and everyone was so pleased to see me back in the circle. They were all talking about ditching the graduation party and going to The SPOT. I hadn't been to The SPOT in months. I agreed to meet them there. I just needed to go home and change my wardrobe. I convinced my mom that I was ready to go and she, herself, was beyond ready to leave. My mom almost never stayed awake past 9:00 pm. As we drove into our driveway, I glanced over at KCs' house. He was still out in the yard with his brothers and friends. I wonder if I had hurt his feelings by trashing his flowers right in his face. *Nah, he has no feelings*, I reminded myself.

I got ready for a night of enjoyment. Just a fun time at The SPOT. I wanted to dance, dance, dance my ass off. Oh, how I just loved to dance. A friend of mine would be by to pick me up any minute now. I slid my body into the shortest shorts ever and a crop top shirt showing all of my perfect slim abdomen. I slid on some all black tennis shoes, because I planned on dancing the soles off tonight. The horn honked for me to come out. I yelled to my mom and Kimber as I ran out the front door, "Be back later, love y'all". As I walked to the car, I heard the men in KCs' yard saying, "Got Damn, she's fine." I thought to myself, *that's right guys remind him what he's missing.*

We arrived at The SPOT and it was already crowded and rocking. As soon as I entered, I joined the dance floor with everyone else. I felt so free. I didn't have a care in the world. It was just me and my dance moves. I made sure to rock my hips and pop my back with every beat to every song. As I was dancing to one of my favorite songs, Maxwell showed up. I said to myself, *please be perfect Maxwell tonight, please come up and dance with me. Just dance, I don't want to talk, I just need for perfect Maxwell to look at me and know exactly what I need*. Without hesitation, that's exactly what Maxwell did. Yes, he can read minds. I was having too much fun right now to worry about Maxwell being too perfect.

The DJ slowed the party down and played a slow song by The Dream, "Falsetto". While it was playing, I was grinding and dipping all over Maxwell. Blowing his mind. Then I felt like someone was watching me. I was pretty sure people were looking already, but this felt like a certain pair of eyes were staring me down. I turned around to place my ass in Maxwell's hands. When I looked over his shoulder, there he was. Standing there with this unsatisfied look in his eyes. It was KC. How did he get in here? Why was he staring me down? I quickly turned around as the song finished and told Maxwell I would see him later. Maxwell stood there and let me go. He didn't chase me or try to figure out why I rushed off. I walked over to Kayla, the girl who I rode with to The Spot and asked her If she was ready to go. She asked me what was wrong, and I told her nothing, that I was just ready to go. She asked me if I could wait for at least 30 minutes more. See, this is exactly why I like to drive myself everywhere I go. When I'm ready to go I don't have to wait for anyone. I told her never mind, I decided to just walk. I didn't live far from THE SPOT but it was a good 20 minute walk. I needed the walk to clear my head anyway.

About 5 minutes into my walk, I began to feel like maybe this was a bad idea. I decided to turn around and catch that ride with Kayla. As I reached the corner of the street, someone snatched me by my hair and pulled me into the dark alley. I was scared and begging for my life. I knew this had been a bad idea. I could feel the person breathing on my neck but he was not saying anything. He still had a hand full of my hair with one hand and put the other hand around my neck. He whispered in my ear to hush before he decided to break my neck. I recognized the voice, it was KC. I calmed down just a little and said to him, “KC, why are you doing this to me?” He tightened the grip around my hair and leaned my head to the side so he could speak directly into my ear and said, “I told you, I want you all to myself.” My heart dropped to my stomach. I was afraid and didn’t know what to do. He turned my body around to face him with one hand still holding my hair. He said to me, “So you think you’re done with me? You’re not done with me until I say you are.” He let go of my hair and gave me the coldest stare before walking off. I gathered myself and exited the alley when Kayla texted me: *Where are you?* I was ready to go, I thought to myself. Perfect timing Kayla.

CHAPTER 10

SHOULD I TELL?

I excited Kayla's car and thanked her for the ride. I was still shook up about what KC did to me, I looked across the street. It was a relief that his car was not there. I walked into the house. It was very dark inside. My mom always left two lights on every night. This was weird. I turned on the light over the stove and then the lamp by the hallway, now I could see. I walked down the hall to the bathroom and took a shower. While I was in the shower, I replayed KC's actions over and over again in my head. He really had lost his mind. I was afraid of him now but I wasn't sure if I should tell anyone. Would anyone believe me? It was not like anyone knew we were messing around besides my sister, Kimber. I had deleted all of his short brief text messages a month ago. No one would believe me with no proof. Not even with Kimber's help, she only knew what I had told her.

I stepped out of the shower with nothing but a towel wrapped around my damped body. I opened the door to my bedroom and reached for the switch to turn my light on. My light was not turning on. I flipped the switch up and down twice more just to be certain. I used the light from my phone to reach the lamp beside my bed. When I reached the lamp and pulled the string to turn it on a hand grabbed me by the neck and began to squeeze. It squeezed me so tight that if I wanted to scream I couldn't. While he had the tight grip of my neck from the back, he said, "Who else have you been fucking?" I recognized his voice immediately. "KC please don't hurt me." I said in return. He repeated the question, this time squeezing a little tighter. I replied, "No one!" He loosened his grip then, but he was still in control. He whispered, "You better not. Or else". I asked him while I still had the chance, "KC, why are you doing this to me?" He looked at me with a daring stare and instead of him responding he took his hand off my neck and slapped me in the back of my head. He forced me down on my bed and removed my towel. I began to cry as he pushed my head into my pillow. The same pillow I once used to scream I hate him in. I'm for sure he was going to rape me now. He yanked me by my hair and told me if I screamed, he would kill me, my mom, and my sister. Afraid that he meant what he said, I covered my mouth with both hands. KC then dug into his pocket and pulled out a condom. He placed the condom on and began to rape me. My body was so tense it was hard for him to enter me, so he forced my legs open wider and pushed himself through. This was very painful. I had never felt so horrible. How could this be happening to me? On this special day. Did I deserve this? 3 minutes later, KC finished and then gathered his things. I lay in my bed curled up like a baby, afraid to move. Before he left, he said to me, "If you tell anyone, no one will believe you." Then he left through my window.

I finally stomached up the energy to go clean myself off. As I walked down the hall to the shower with my robe on my entire body was shaking. He raped me. He raped me. I showered again trying to wash him off of me. I sobbed in the shower with every scrub. I couldn't get him off of me. Finally, tired of letting the water drip in my face, I exited the shower and dried off. I was too afraid to go to my room tonight. I slid on the pajamas that I brought with me to the shower and instead of going back to my room, I went into Kimber's room to sleep with her. Kimber and my mom are deep sleepers. Even if I had screamed, I'm not sure if they would have heard me.

As I laid there in Kimber's bed, she didn't even realize that I was beside her. I forced myself to think about something else. I did not want to relive what just happened to me. I didn't want to have any nightmares, only good dreams that night. I closed my eyes super tight and tried to erase KC's face. His face kept appearing with every squint and his words kept echoing in my brain. I couldn't sleep. I laid beside Kimber, hoping that she would wake up without me shaking her. Kimber was having sweet dreams, who was I to disturb her with this mess that I had caused. I knew that this was my fault, all of the flirting and pursuing. This older man whom I barely knew. I knew I had to leave here, so that he wouldn't hurt me or my family. I had not planned on leaving for college until winter. I needed to call the administrator to see if it was too late to enroll for summer classes. Once I knew that I had somewhat of an escape plan, sooner rather than later, I was finally able to fall asleep.

I woke up the next morning to the smell of bacon. My mom was cooking breakfast, but I didn't have an appetite. I rolled over to see Kimber's face, but she was not there. How had I not felt Kimber move? She must have slithered her way out of the bed, not wanting to wake me. I exited Kimber's room and headed to the bathroom to brush my teeth. With the bathroom door open, I could hear my mom and a deep voice talking. I quickly rinsed my mouth with mouthwash and walked down the hall to the living room. Standing in my living room was KC. My heart started to pound through my chest. I stood there wondering what his next move was. KC looked at me and smiled. My mom said to me, "Dynver Girl, what's wrong with you? Why are you standing there looking like a deer in headlights?" *Oh momma, if you only knew the devil is standing in your living room*. "Go finish washing up, KC only stopped by to give you a graduation gift." I replied, "Yes, Ma'am" and returned to the bathroom to wash my face. Why was he hunting me? Was he trying to make sure I stayed quiet? And where the hell was Kimber? I returned to the living room and KC was still standing there. He smiled at me and told me congrats on graduating while he handed me an envelope. I said thank you while I was receiving the envelope. I did not make eye contact. My mom thought this was a sweet thing he did for me. She was clueless. She was not even asking herself why a grown man was making it his duty to give me, her teenage daughter, a graduation gift. KC left after having a few more words with my mom. I sat at the kitchen table with food on my plate but was not really hungry enough to eat.

My mom entered the kitchen and with this surprised look on her face she asked, "So what does the card say?" I opened the envelope with disgust and then slid the card out of the envelope. The front of the card said, 'Congrats Graduate'. When I opened the card, money fell out. Twenty funky dollars. Was this all I was worth? Really? My mom, over the top excited for me, said, "GOD is Good". I looked at my mom and without thinking I said, "God don't have nothing to do with this." My mom, unsure of why I was irritated, asked me, "Dynver, what's wrong?" I looked my mom in her eyes. I decided I was just going to tell her. She was my mom and she would know what to do. She would not let anyone hurt her babies. Instead, I said, "Nothing Mom. I'm just menstrual this morning. Where's Kimber?" My mom looked back to me with concern and a stare that said she doesn't believe me. My mom, much like Kimber, would only harass me for answers when she was tired of waiting. My mom responded, “Kimber got up early this morning to help me with some errands. She should be back any second now. She told me you were sleeping in her room. What possessed you to do that, Dynver?” I wanted to tell her the truth so badly, but I also wanted her and Kimber to remain safe. All of KC’s actions within the last 24 hours proved to me that I need to take him seriously. I told my mom I just couldn’t sleep well in my bed last night after having a bad dream. By the look on her face, she still did not believe me, and I had about one more lie to tell before she had enough. Before I left the kitchen table, she asked me one more question, “What happened to your light bulb?” I looked at my mom, knowing this was my final lie and said, “I don’t know.”

CHAPTER 11

I’VE GOT TO DO SOMETHING

Kimber finally arrived back home from running errands for Mom. I sent her a text message to meet me in my room. When Kimber entered my room, I told her to shut the door, be quiet, and just listen. Kimber nervously did as I asked and then she sat on the edge of my bed. I had taken everything off my bed. The sheets and comforter were removed and rolled up together on the floor in a corner. The five pillows that I used to decorate my bed were now scattered over the floor. I wish I could just throw the entire bed away with no questions asked. I began to tell Kimber everything that happened and the look on her face showed a mixture of fear and pisstivity. Kimber sat there quietly for all of two seconds and then said, "We need to tell MOM!" Her voice echoed a little bit louder than what I expected, being that I told her to be quiet. I gave her a serious look and said, "Kimber, keep your voice down. I don't want to tell Mom. Didn't you hear what I told you he said? If I tell anyone he will kill us all. I'm not sure he's bluffing. I just want to disappear before things get worse. You have to promise me you will not tell Mom or anyone else." Kimber stared into my eyes with her own now filled with tears and said, "What do we do now?" I told Kimber I didn't know but I would figure it out. I could tell Kimber desperately wanted to tell Mom, I just prayed she wouldn't.

Kimber gave me a tight hug and whispered in my ear, "I love you!" She gathered herself together, the best that she could, so it would not seem like something was wrong when she was around Mom. Kimber was nothing like me when being questioned by Mom. Normally, if Mom noticed something wrong with Kimber and asked her what's wrong, Kimber would pour all her feelings out. I just prayed and hoped, since it was not her business to share, that she would learn how to keep it together this once. For me at least. I had to do something about this room and especially the bed. I took the comforter and sheets and put them in the washer. I would never use them on my bed ever again. I then took the pillows and threw them in the laundry room. I changed my room around to block KC from being able to enter through my window. I moved the bed closer to the bedroom door. The dresser with the mirror blocked the entire window, I guess this was goodbye natural light. I moved the lamp right next to the entrance of the door, so I did not have to walk across the room just to turn it on. *You will not attack me again in the dark*, I said to myself.

After I finished changing my room around, I was exhausted. I laid across the new sheets and comforter set that we kept in the linen closet in the hallway. Although the sheets and the comforter smelled fresh and my room was changed around, the memory of what happened to me here still felt the same. I was honestly still in disbelief all of this happened, and I didn't know what to expect next. I thought I should text him and ask why he was doing this to me. I needed answers but I was too afraid that I would only make him upset and I would still not have an answer. As I was laying on my bed with my face to the ceiling, staring at the replaced light bulb, I heard his car pull up in his driveway. I walked over to the now blocked window and peeped through the side of it to get a glimpse of him. I wanted to see the person he is in the daylight. I wanted to see if he looked like the monster he is at night. He got out of the car and sat on the porch with his brothers. He was laughing and smiling, as if he had done nothing wrong. Since I could watch his reaction, I decided to do it. I was going to ask him why. I texted the words and my brain wanted to press the send button, but my fingers would not follow the order. I was too afraid to piss him off.

I erased the message and walked away from the window. Maybe he would just leave me alone if I stayed out of his sight. If he didn't see me then he would just forget all about me. This should be interesting. How could I possibly stay out of his sight? I lived right across the street and the town was small. I guess it was time to call the administrator at Florida State University to see if I could move into the dorm for summer semester.

CHAPTER 12

THE ESCAPE

With the new way my room was set up and the new sheets and comforter, I thought I would be able to at least close my eyes in my room. Every time I closed my eyes, my heart started pounding. It was as if he was standing over me, waiting to do it to me all over again. I thought back to the very first time I met him, and I questioned, *Did I do this to myself? Is there any way possible I could have known he was a rapist, better yet, a psycho killer rapist?* Maybe him not having much to say should have been my red flag. My mom had always told us, it was the quiet people you have to watch out for. I took his quietness as cuteness though. Urgh, I was not going to be able to get a decent night sleep here. I guess I would just sleep with Kimber again.

Kimber woke me up the next morning and asked me if I was ok. I looked at her with my morning face, one eye opened and one eye closed and said, "I've definitely been better." Kimber told me, "If you don't want mom to ask any questions you should start back sleeping in your room." She was right. If mom noticed I was not sleeping in my room, she would definitely question it. I told Kimber thank you and slid out of her bed. I entered my room and I took a look around to see if anything had been moved. Everything was still in place. I could not live like this. Paranoia would not be my new best friend. I looked through my dresser drawer for the envelope with information to contact the administrator so I could inquire about the enrollment for summer semester. I typed the email and pressed the send button. My fingers followed the orders from my brain, finally.

I could not stay cooped up in this house like this for much longer. I needed the sun to touch my skin. If I stepped outside of these walls, then he would surely see me and want more of me. I could not have that happen. Maybe I could just sit on my porch and enjoy that for now. If I saw or heard his car pulling up, I would just run back inside. Literally, run. *Here goes nothing*. I walked down the hall with my legs shaking with each nervous step I took. I reached the door and placed my hand on the door handle and opened it. I looked across the street to make sure the coast was clear. His car was not there, I was good to go. I stepped on the porch and had a seat in my favorite chair. It felt good. I was listening to the birds' chirp and watching the cars ride up and down the street. I moved my chair a little closer to the door entrance, so when I saw or heard his car coming, I could quickly enter my home without him getting a glimpse of my shadow.

A brand new car with the dealership tag still on it pulled up in my driveway. My heart dropped to my gut. It was a black 2005 Dodge Charger with a very dark tint. The tint was so dark, I don't believe the person on the inside should be able to look out. I sat there with my gut bubbling. If this was him, I didn't want to do anything to make him mad. The driver side of the dark tinted car window rolled down slowly. It was Maxwell. Oh my God, he scared the crap out of me. I was happy to see his face, and not the other creep. I walked off my porch and towards Maxwell's new car. He was smiling at me and I was smiling back at him. Just like the perfect gentleman he was, he exited his car and greeted me with a gentle hug. He asked me why I had not been returning his texts or calls. I told him that I was just stressed about the new life after high school and needed time to myself. He believed me, I guess. I asked him questions about the new car and like normal, we carried a good conversation all about school and careers and future beach life for me. The conversation was so intense I forgot that I should be hiding in the house before the predator comes home from wherever it was that he went when I used to look for him. I heard the car, and saw his car pull into his driveway all slow motion like. My eyes locked in on him. I couldn't breathe right now. I could hear Maxwell talking but my brain couldn't process the words. KC got out of his car and leaned against it with his eyes staring me down. He was not smiling. I could see every nerve in his face. I was his property, I reminded myself. Maxwell was still talking, and I still didn't know what he was saying. My mind was so focused on KC and what he was thinking at that moment. I had to get out of there.

Maxwell finally took a break from chatting and asked me if I would like to ride in his new car. If I got in the car with him, it would surely piss KC off. I had been watching KC stare at me while talking to Maxwell and could see he was definitely already pissed. I told Maxwell I had something to do for my mom and I would have to wait till next time for the car ride. Maxwell said he understood, but the look on his face read that he was bummed. He then took my hand and pulled me in close to him to give me a hug. I hugged him back, but it didn't feel the same with KC stabbing me in my back with his eyes. I walked toward my door and Maxwell honked his horn at me as he was leaving out of my driveway. Quickly, I ran into the house and locked the door.

What should I do? What should I do? I thought to myself. I paced my bedroom floor out of anxiousness that KC would attack me soon, I just didn't know when. I decided I was about ready to let my mom know what was really going on. I couldn't handle this by myself anymore. I didn't want to live in fear. I peeped out the side of the curtain to see if he was still sitting there. He was still there. Oh my, should I text him and let him know Maxwell is just a friend and please don't hurt me? My phone was in my hand and my heart was beating faster and faster to where it seemed like it was about to explode. My phone binged. Afraid that he had texted me before I got a chance to explain, I dropped the phone out of panic. I sat for a while nervous to see what he texted. I picked the phone up and it was an email notification from Ms Clarke at FSU. Yes, some good news. I could enroll for the summer semester. Although it was good news, I still had two more weeks before I could move in. How was I going to manage to stay clear of KC for 2 weeks?

I was sleeping in my room that night with one eye closed and one eye definitely open. The lamp was on, my mom's electricity bill was going to be sky high. I heard a noise by my window. I didn't dare move or breathe. A text message was sent to my phone, it was KC. The message said for me to meet him in his garage. He claims he wants to talk and apologize. I don't believe him for one second. I heard the noise by the window again. Afraid that it was KC, I quickly ran out of my bedroom door and into my mom's room. I woke her up by pushing her and screaming mom. She woke up alarmed and asked me what was wrong. I told her someone is outside my window. My mom grabbed her bat that she kept near the bed and we walked into my room. As she was creeping closer to my window, the noise of someone's footsteps by my window was heard by the both of us. My mom peeped through the side of the curtain to get a glance of who could possibly be outside of my window when exclaimed, "Dynver girl, it's just a cat!" I was relieved it was a cat instead of the worst thing that it could ever be, which was KC. I didn't go see KC nor did I reply. I was certain he was going to reply or send another text threatening me, but he didn't. Was it over? Was he done with me? The next two weeks went by slowly, I stayed in the house and avoided his every appearance. He didn't text or call and it almost felt like I was free. He had forgotten about me. Yet I was left with wondering, maybe he had really wanted to apologize and I had not given him the opportunity to make things right.

CHAPTER 13

THE BEACH

Watch out Florida here I come. I was smiling from ear to ear while loading up my car to drive to FSU. Kimber, whom I thought would be sad of my leaving, was loading my car quicker than Speedy Gonzales. She was probably just happy for me to go and get away from KC. She had not been the same with me since promising to keep my secret. My mom was excited for me as well, but of course for a totally different reason than Kimber. My mom has always wanted for her girls to travel and see the world just like she had done when she was just a young tenderoni. I was too excited to give KC another thought. I didn't even look across the street to see if he was there to watch me drive off. I gave my mom and sister a hug and a kiss on the cheeks and told them I will call them when I arrive.

The entire ride, I took the time to set rules for myself so that I would never place myself in the same toxic situation. I made sure to advise myself to stay focused on my schoolwork and stay out of trouble. I listened to gospel music to keep my spirits high and in the right place. After my gospel music had lifted me higher than ever, I turned on some of that Hip Hop and R&B vibe so that I could vibe the rest of the way. Finally, I was here, I had arrived at FSU. Everything felt good and new. I entered the school and met up with Ms. Clarke to have the full tour and be shown to my dorm.

After Ms. Clarke showed me where I would be staying, she advised me that orientation would be in about 3 hours. I should have more than enough time to start moving my things from my car to my dorm. I returned to my dorm room and just took it all in. My roommate had decided to wait until winter semester to move in. So I would have this space all to myself for a few more months. I began to walk back and forth to my dorm, unloading my car. While I was unloading the car, I noticed a car much like KC's. I paused, thinking to myself, *did he really follow me here just to finally hurt me?* As the car drove by, my breathing resumed, it was not KC. I told myself, *Dynver girl, you have got to stop being so darn paranoid.*

Finally, I was finished with unloading so it was time to do some unpacking. I hated unpacking just as much as I hated folding the clothes and putting them away once they're done drying. I began unpacking and midway through I wondered how far the beach is away from my dorm and if I had time to make it there and back. I loved the beach, just seeing it always helped me settle in a bit faster. I grabbed my phone and searched for the nearest beach. The nearest beach was about 30 minutes away from the school. I still had two hours before orientation. I was sure I could make it there and back. I stopped unpacking and rode to the beach.

When I arrived the first thing I heard was the ocean. It was beyond comforting already. I took my sandals off to walk through the beach sand. Every step felt lighter and lighter. I spread my arms out as I took it all in. The scenery sparkled in front of my eyes. The sound of the seagulls and the ocean played soothing music in my ear. The feel of the sand that was sinking between my toes. "I'm here, I'm here", I chanted out loud. I could sit there all day, with an umbrella of course, the sunlight was not in agreement with my forehead that day. As I took it all in, it dawned on me, I forgot to call Kimber and Mom to let them know of my safe arrival. I gave them a call as I was walking back to my car. Mom sounded so proud of me and asked me questions about the view and reminded me again for the millionth time the do's and don'ts while I was here. Then I saw the car that reminded me of KC's car again. I knew it was not him but I just got so paranoid when I saw that car.

I arrived at orientation right on time. Everyone seemed happy and in good spirits. There were different types of people that I was going to get to know. The school was very diverse, unlike the small town I was from. I've never seen a large group of people filled with different cultures at the same time. I was just beyond excited to learn new things in life. I walked back to my dorm room to finish the unpacking. While unpacking I noticed a red shoe box that I had not noticed before. I wondered if it was a bomb KC had planted in my car to kill me off. You can never be so sure. Especially since I had not expected him to do any of the things he did. I just wished I could forget about him as if it never happened. I was in another state and yet I felt like he was still haunting me. I opened the shoe box and inside was a note and pictures. Pictures of Kimber, Mom, and me with a short note from Kimber. Her note read, "Dear Dynver, We love you. Life isn't always picture perfect but in these pictures they are. Love, Mom and Kimber." They have always surprised me with little things like this to brighten my day. It was the simple things in life that gave the greatest motivation. I made a promise to myself, right then and there, I would not continue to live this paranoid life.

Thoughts of KC haunting me would not be a part of my life anymore.

CHAPTER 14

KANNON

I had been enjoying college life for three weeks now. I must say this was life. I did not have to hear my mom complaining about dishes, clothes, or any of the other things she normally complained about. Although I did miss her cooking. The school food could use some flavor. I had met some cool and down to earth people within a couple of weeks of me being there. Everyone was about having fun and focusing on their school studies at the same time. The environment was much different than high school. It might have been because everyone was focused on the same goals (for the most part): Complete four years of college and head to the real world while having sprinkles of fun here and there.

It was Friday night and two of my new friends, Mya and Amber, invited me to a birthday for this guy named Kannon. Kannon was the starting quarterback for the Florida State Seminoles. He was about 6'3" and 230 lbs. His chocolate skin was so perfectly smooth. His arms and chest muscles screamed out to me, "Hercules! Hercules!" Handsomely complimented, yes indeed. Oh, and I could not forget about those pearly whites. His teeth sparkled with every smile. This man was definitely eye candy. Which was all he could be for me. My new rule for myself was not to seduce anyone and to let things happen as naturally as possible. Playing the seduce him game had not worked out for me at all.

Mya and Amber arrived at my dorm eagerly ready to get to the party. They waited impatiently as I put the final touches of my outfit together. It was not as risky as I used to dress. I was wearing blue jean shorts and a nice fitted FSU tee-shirt. To add just a little bit of flavor to my outfit, I accessorized it with ankle bracelets to compliment my legs, earrings to add attention to my face, and wrist bracelets because it was the trend for now. My feet were still perfectly pedicured with white toenail polish. I had hung out at small dorm gatherings with them, but I had yet to have attended an actual party. I really had not done much dancing lately, but I'm sure my body would remember what it was supposed to do when the beat drops.

We arrived at the party on time. This was new to me since I normally arrive fashionably late. I looked around and I could literally count how many people were present. The music was playing, and the few people there were vibing with each other. Back home this would normally mean the party was lame and everyone had gone to the cool party. Either way, I did not care how many people were there. When my body heard a familiar song I could groove to, it would be to the dance floor I'll go. Mya and Amber both looked disappointed and turned to me and said, "No one is here." I looked at my watch and told them, "It's 9:30 PM, most people probably won't start arriving until 10:00 pm or later." Mya and Amber were both from the same small town in Tennessee. They were besties who decided to get as far away as possible from their strict parents. I was kind of like their leader, showing them the ropes when I barely knew the ropes myself. I guess I was just more experienced than they were so they look to me for guidance.

I excused myself to run to the Ladies room. On the way to the restroom I received a text message on my phone from a random number not saved in my phone. With confusion written all over my face, before I could open the text message, boom, I walked completely into this beautiful human. Kannon. They say don't text and drive, but I think they need to acknowledge how unsafe it is to text and walk too. Kannon asked me if I was ok. Without hesitation, I responded by telling him yes. He asked for my name and just like that I quickly forgot I had to use the restroom. I was totally ready to flirt. I forgot all the rules I set for myself and the seducing began. I stared into his eyes, knowing what my eyes were capable of, and said, "Dynver". He introduced himself to me while holding my hand for a greeter's handshake and said, "Nice of you to walk into my arms Ms Dynver. I'm Kannon." His response with a smile gave me flirt vibes. I apologized for bumping into him and carried on to the bathroom. He had my heart pumping with excitement. I couldn't wait to get to know him on a more personal level. I left the restroom and met up with Mya and Amber at the punch bowl. Uhoh, there it was, the DJ was playing my song. I was already feeling like my old self and my body was following the beat. I grabbed Mya and Amber by the hand and we hit the dance floor. Dancing felt so normal for me. I felt like Dynver again, not the girl with a lot of rules for herself. Perhaps it was okay for me to still do and be the things that make me who I am without getting myself into any relationship trouble.

While me and the girls were dancing and having a good time, I noticed a set of my eyes on me. I could feel their eyes all over me. They started from my hips and worked their way up my spine. I continued to dance freely while smiling with enjoyment. Then I connected with the eyes that were watching me. It was Kannon. He was watching me with satisfaction. I stared into his eyes as I continued to dance. Kannon started walking my way. What was he doing? This was not a part of the plan. Kannon, now standing in front of me, watched me up close. Without asking, he grabbed my waist and pulled me close to him and we began to dance. I did not reject him, and I thought to myself, remember, let things happen naturally. All night Kannon and I just danced and danced.

When the party was over Kannon walked me out to Amber's car. Mya and Amber were patiently waiting on me with smiles on their faces. I knew they had a thousand questions for me. I told Kannon thank you for walking me to the car and Happy Birthday. Kannon, with a smile on his face, opened the door for me and once I was safely in, shut the door. He started to walk away and then quickly turned around and asked me for my number. Wow, it was much easier to let things happen naturally. Later that night, I remembered I didn't check the text message I was about to open when I bumped into Kannon. I looked at the message again and I was still unsure of who the number belonged to. I decided it wasn't worth reading and I deleted the message.

CHAPTER 15

HE'S LOOKING FOR ME

Kannon and I had considered ourselves dating since his birthday party. These past three weeks with him had been awesome. He asked all the right questions and said all the flirty little things I like to hear. I did not have to do anything special to keep his attention. He took me out on what he calls a chill ice cream date at his favorite ice cream shop. We sat and talked and laughed all chill like. I let him know all the things I like to do. It was a total vibe when we were together. Kannon reminded me of Maxwell, but not so much. It was something about getting all the things you wanted from a person, but them not being the person you want it from. That was what Maxwell was to me. He was doing all the right things, but he just wasn't the guy I wanted it from.

Five weeks away from home. I officially felt like I was grown and could take care of myself. With the assistance of the weekly allowance my mom agreed to send me every week, of course. Everything was feeling and looking good for me. Kannon texted me a message that read: *Good Morning beautiful. After class today I have a surprise for you, so meet me at my car right after*. I read his message and just felt all warm inside. I couldn't wait to see what he had planned for me. Kannon had truly been God sent. In the short time of knowing him, he brightened up my world. I had completely forgotten about KC and the thought of him hunting me.

After class I rushed to meet Kannon. I arrived at his car and he was not there. Ok, this was weird. What was happening to my perfect guy? He knew what time he told me to meet him. He knew what time I got out of class. Where the freak was he? Kannon was the type of guy I would wait all day for. It had been about five minutes of me waiting and I was starting to get anxious. Then there he was, Mr. Kannon, jogging towards his car. He reached me then gave me a tight hug and apologized for being late. I didn't question him. He opened the door for me and jogged to the driver side. He looked me in my eyes and apologized once more before we drove off to the secret location. About 5 minutes before we arrived, I knew where he was taking me. He brought me to my favorite place to be, the beach. I smiled and he smiled back at me. He parked the car and said, "Well we're here". He opened my door and then walked to the trunk of the car. He opened the trunk and he had a picnic basket with drinks and food. I stood there knowing I deserved this. I deserved to be cherished like this. We walked on the beach and found a special place to set up.

We sat with our toes buried in the sand and just talked and laughed with each other. He brought grapes, chips, and sub sandwiches with water bottles for us to drink. He was such a dude but it was the thought that counted. After we finished eating, we went for a beach walk. Kannon placed his hand around my waist as we walked. He then stopped walking and turned me to him. He looked me in my eyes and started to lean in to kiss me. We kissed. This was our first kiss since we had started dating. It was a long kiss too. I stood there in his arms allowing him to caress my body with his hands and kiss me from my lips to my neck then back to my lips again. The kissing got so heated, my hormones began to wake up. I needed to keep them asleep for as long as I could. I stopped kissing Kannon and smiled at him, giving him the look of, *Ok that's enough for now*. He understood without speaking and we continued our walk.

We strolled back to the picnic area and gathered our things. We were walking back to his car smiling and holding hands, when I noticed the car that looked like KC's car in the parking lot. Although the car reminded me of KC's car, I was not nervous or afraid this time. I knew it was not him. It had been five weeks, I'm sure he had forgotten about me. Kannon and I spoke about the party he was hosting the upcoming weekend. He asked me for help setting up and I agreed. Kannon's life consisted of four things right now, which was: school, football, partying and oh yeah, ME. Kannon enjoyed his time with me just as much as I enjoyed my time with him.

We arrived back at the school and Kannon gave me a hug and a kiss on the cheek. My body screamed for his pleasant touch, but I reminded myself that I was in control. I would not give my body up so easily, KC taught me that. Although I felt like Kannon would not be anything like KC, I still felt it was best I make him wait. Kannon walked me to my dorm and we said goodnight. I was so happy with how my life was going right now. I couldn't wait to update Kimber about me and Kannon. As I was getting my clothes together to take a shower, an unknown number sent a text message to my phone. Who could it be? I didn't know if it was the same unknown number that texted me once before. I opened the text message curious to see who it was and what they could possibly want. The message read: *Do you miss me?* I replied back: *Who is this?* With a quick response a text message was sent back to me: *You will see soon*. I got nervous. Could this be him? It couldn't be.

Did he change his number? I still had his number saved so that I would be able to ignore him.

Someone knocked on my door. My heart pounding with fear, I said, “Who is it?”. “It’s me, Amber.” My entire body exhaled with relief. I opened the door to let Amber in and standing beside her was KC. My eyes widened and I could see my life flash before me. Amber held KC’s hand and entered my room. She was smiling and staring at KC as if he was something to look at. I remained quiet until she said, “Dynver, this is KC.” I wanted to tell her I knew exactly who he was, and she should run. She continued, “We’ve been seeing each other for three weeks now and I wanted him to meet all my close friends.” She was rambling on and on at this point and I had tuned her out. I was having conversations in my head about how I should tell her who he really was and what he really did to me. I tune back into her talking right at the point when she said, “Oh yeah guess what? He’s from the same city you’re from”. KC stood there in my dorm room acting like the perfect gentleman and had the nerve to open his mouth and say, “What street did you live on?” I didn’t know how to answer and before I could answer, Amber who apparently knew all my business except for this one thing answered for me. She was overly excited to showboat him around. He then said to me, “We stayed on the same street. What a small world. I don't remember seeing you". I said back to him, with an attitude in my voice, "I never met you either." I told Amber that I felt tired and I had to get some rest and rushed them out of my room. The nerve, the nerve, the nerve of him. I had to warn Amber's gullible ass. I could show her the previous text messages and just tell her everything but if he changed his number then I couldn't prove to her that it was him. I didn't have any pictures of me and him together and I basically just lied as if I never met him. She should believe me, right? I could show her the messages he sent before they walked into my room. What if that was not the number he gave her? I did not want to lose a friend. Why is KC trying to interrupt my life right now? I was sure I left him back in Georgia.

I sat and thought of how long Amber said she's been seeing KC and figured out KC has been here for at least three weeks. That means it was him at the beach today. He was watching me this entire time. Bing! It was a text message on my phone from the same unknown number. I now knew it was KC. The message read: *It was good seeing you tonight.* I didn't reply, I had to tell someone before KC attacked me. Who could I trust? The way Amber had been looking at KC, I'm sure she felt like she was in love and there was a strong possibility she may think I was hating. I don't want to tell Kannon because I'm too embarrassed to say how I seduced my way into a psycho rapist's arms. I don't want Kannon to look at me differently. I don't know what else to do. Please, please just leave me alone KC.

CHAPTER 16

THE GIRLFRIEND

I didn't get much sleep that night. I tried to plan out how I could get rid of KC without involving anyone. I really needed to talk to Amber. Maybe I could find out more information of what he might have told her and find a way to convince her to leave him without giving her all the information. My thoughts were all over the place. Kannon texted me:

Good morning beautiful, just like he did every morning. I smiled when I read it but then before I could reply to him, the unknown number texted again. Urgh, KC please go back to Georgia. I opened the message and it said for me to meet him by my car. I felt so alone right now. If I told anyone about him harassing me I felt like I would be the one in the wrong. Why did I feel like this? I knew he was the one in the wrong. Why did I feel like I was not the victim?

I didn't reply to KC and I didn't show up to my car. I knew I had pissed him off but I needed time to think how I could get rid of him. The entire time during my class, I couldn't focus. Kannon texted me that he wouldn't be able to meet me after class today. Something happened at football practice and he would tell me about it later. Now what should I do? I texted Amber and Mya to see what they were doing after class and if we could hangout? Amber replied back that she would be with her new boo, KC of course. Mya would be hanging out with her new boo too. Everyone would be snuggled up after class except for me. Well, at least KC would be too occupied with Amber, so I guess that could give me a little more time to think of what to do.

I returned to my dorm room after class. Although I knew KC would be with Amber, I felt much safer inside than out today. I texted Kannon letting

him know I would be waiting on his call and I hoped everything was ok. Why was this happening right now? I laid on my bed waiting for Kannon's phone call and then there was a knock at my door. I quickly opened it thinking it was Kannon but was not him, it was Amber. "Hey Amber, I thought you were going to be too busy to chill today." I said to her while she was standing at the door and looking behind her to see If KC was anywhere in sight. Amber let herself into my room and said, "Yeah, but KC cancelled on me at the last minute". Uh-oh, I thought to myself, he must be somewhere planning something evil. I wanted to have a girl talk with Amber and ask her questions like how did you meet? And what were his conversations like and had they kissed yet. Normal questions friends would ask, but I was too focused on what KC might have up his sleeves. Unable to be the real friend I needed to be to Amber right now, I told her I had to meet up with Kannon to discuss something very important and that I would catch up with her later.

On my way to Kannon's dorm to wait on him there, I gave him a call to see if he was still busy. He didn't answer. I sent him a text letting him know I would be waiting for him in the lobby by his dorm. He didn't reply. Maybe he was too busy to reply. I sat in the lobby looking like a lonely lost puppy. Where the hell was Kannon? And why hadn't he responded to any of my calls or texts? Finally, I saw him walk in and I ran to him and placed my body in his arms. "Why didn't you respond to me? I was worried about you." Kannon's body seemed cold and distant. He looked down at me and said, "They suspended me off the team." "What! Why?" That's when Kannon let me know someone planted marijuana and other drugs in his locker and he has no way to prove it wasn't his so for now he is suspended until further investigation. I thought I knew how it got there but I didn't know how that would help him right now. That would mean I would have to share my embarrassing secret story in hopes that everyone would understand and take the risk of losing everyone if none of them understand. I was not ready to lose Kannon right now.

I sat with Kannon the rest of the night, telling him that everything would work out while rubbing his back. Kannon looked at me with this daze in his eyes as if he was searching for stress relief. I know what he wanted but right now was definitely not the perfect time for our first time. I removed my hands from rubbing his back and whispered in his ear, "I have to go." Kannon respectfully said okay and walked me to the door. *Well that was too easy*, I said to myself. He didn't even ask why? Or try to fight for me to stay. I was feeling like I should've stayed and given him exactly what he needed right then and there. I puzzled this out while walking towards my dorm. I couldn't decide if I should turn around and give Kannon all of me, all of my goods to help him through this tough time because technically it was my fault. If he hadn't been interested in me, KC would have never planted those drugs in his locker. I knew KC did it, no one else would want to hurt Kannon. I decided not to return to Kannon's dorm and to let him just sleep it off. I hope he was not upset with me.

As I was walking towards my dorm I heard a soft voice call my name, "Dynver". I didn't think it could be KC because the voice sounded like a female. I turned to try and find who could be calling my name. They called my name again, then flashed their car headlights my way.

Who the heck was this? I walked towards the car and to my surprise I recognized the face. It was KC's girlfriend. I remembered her face from watching her from across the street. What could she want with me and how did she know my name? She could tell from the look on my face that I knew exactly who she was. She asked me to get in the car quickly and that we needed to talk. Hearing the urgency in her voice, I did just that. Once I was inside her car, she started the car up and drove off. "Hey Lady!" Where the hell are you taking me?" She looked at me and said, "I'm not here to hurt you but I am here to warn you. I'm taking you to my hotel where we can talk safely." She was here to warn me about KC. Well I didn't need a warning, I needed help.

CHAPTER 17

KEEP RUNNING

We arrived at her hotel and before we exited the vehicle, she looked over at me and said, “Are you ok?” I responded to her by nodding my head yes. We left the car and entered the hotel. She seemed so calm yet nervous at the same time. I’m not sure why I felt like I could trust her. What if she was a part of all of this and I had fallen for the trap? Oh Lord, please don’t let this be a trap. While we were on the elevator I asked her, “What's your name?” She looked at me and responded with a soft voice, “Marissa”. The elevator dinged and we were on the 7th floor. Welp, it was officially too high for me to jump off the building if I needed to. We walked down the hall to Marissa’s room. There goes my heart again, pulsating through my skin. Why did I put myself in life or death situations? When we arrived at room number 715, I thought to myself, *well this is the end of Dynver Irene Hartage*. Marissa was about to open this door and behind this lucky door would be KC standing there ready to end me.

Marissa opened the door and I followed behind her. She sat on the bed and told me to have a seat. I followed her orders, but my brain was still waiting for KC to pop out of the bathroom, closet, or even under the bed somewhere. I looked at her and I said, “So what is it you have to warn me about?” Marissa stared into my eyes and responded with a serious tone, “I know you were dealing with KC during the same time me and him were in a relationship”. What, wait they’re not in a relationship anymore? Is this why he was still interested in me? Please take him back Marissa.

She continued, “KC was really good to me and then he started to change. He became distant and violent. When he would come over to spend the night with me the sex would be different. It would be rougher than the way I liked it. Then there was this one night I decided to stay the night over at his house. While I was in his bedroom waiting for him to come home from work, I got bored and decided to watch a movie. I placed an unknown DVD in his DVD player and the video that played was a video of you and him. I knew that was all the information I needed to see that he was messing around on me, but I continued to look for more evidence that he was seeing you. I stumbled across this box of personals. In the box were panties, bras, hair and used condoms. It looked like it could've belonged to multiple women because the strands of hair were tied separately. When he arrived home that night I questioned him about the DVD and the box. He pulled me by my hair to the floor and got on top of me and whispered in my ear that he would kill me if I ever snooped through his things again. I had never seen this side of him and I was afraid of the next thing he would do. I apologized to him for going through his things and I thought that once I apologized he would loosen his grip on my hair but instead he tightened his grip and pulled me up. He stared into my eyes while the tears rolled down my face and placed his free hand around my neck and began to squeeze. He said to me as I was trying to pull his hand from around my neck, "Be still or I will break it". I calmed down and he threw me onto his bed. He told me to get undressed and at this point I was following his every command. I cried as I removed my clothing while he was standing there watching. He told me to shut up with the crying and removed his belt. He told me to turn over on my stomach, and when I turned over, KC did the unthinkable. He punished me with his belt like I was his child. I screamed for help with each lick he gave me but no one heard me. He pressed his knee into my back and wrapped the belt around my neck. I struggled with him to try and fight him back but he overpowered me and pulled my neck with the belt. He told me that if I move an inch off the bed when he lets me go that he will kill me. He got off the bed, I didn't turn around but I could hear him rip something open. He told me to turn over. I watched him put the condom on and he climbed on top of me. He opened my legs and then grabbed the belt and pulled my face towards him and before he entered me he said: 'You are mine just like she is mine. And if you try to go to the police about any of this I will burn all the evidence you think you seen and when they question me I will just tell them we're going through a bad break up. Once they leave I will find you and I will kill you.' I believed him, I left his house that day confused. I decided to just ignore him but everywhere I looked he was there. Then I found out from his cousin Derrick that KC was moving to Florida so I was so filled with relief. I thought to myself, finally, he has moved on and I could be free, but then he sends me a text letting me know that he was going to come and visit you and once he finds you he would come back for me and that we all would be together here in Florida. I knew then I had to do something. I came to warn you of what type of person he is. I know you're young and you may think it's true love but it's not. He's very abusive and you need to be careful. I sat there and stared into Marissa's face. Tears were rolling down her cheeks as she told me her story and tears were rolling down my cheeks because I feared this only happened to her because of me. I blamed myself for all of it. If only I hadn't pursued KC none of this would be happening right now. I knew it was time to share with Marissa what happened with me and KC.

I spilled all my troubles of dealing with KC out to Marissa. This was the first time I had shared this with anyone other than Kimber. Then

I told Marissa that KC is already here in Florida and about what he was doing with Amber and Kannon. She agreed with me that we must do something, but KC had manipulated us both into believing that there was nothing we could do to him. She didn't know if anyone would believe us, especially since he would deny being involved with me and he would make it seem like she's the bitter ex-girlfriend. In addition to all of that, we were both too embarrassed to let anyone else know what happened especially if they were not going to believe us.

Marissa and I sat in her room silently for the next 20 minutes then she said, "I got it!" I sat up hoping that she may actually have the answer to help us both out of this predicament alive. She told me the plan of how were going to trap KC and have him arrested for sexual abuse. I listened to her plan and the plan is mostly about everything that she was going to do and then she said to me, "But, you're going to have to call him and meet up with him alone." I quickly said, "NO! I do not and will not be alone anywhere with him." She said to me this is the only way to get rid of KC for his wrong doings to us. I told her again "NO!" Marissa looked at me with a disappointed stare. I told her I didn't know what we're going to do but leaving me alone with him would not be a part of the plan. I then told Marissa that it was getting too late and that I should return to my dorm now. I assured her that I would meet up with her tomorrow to come up with another plan. Marissa agreed and took me back to my dorm.

We arrived at the school parking lot and waited for any signs of KC before I left the car. I gave Marissa my number and told her to call me to let me know when she returned to the hotel safely. I exited the car and when I did, I could feel his eyes on me. My knees got weak as I stood beside Marissa's car knowing he's watching. I searched around the parking lot to see If I could see him before he could attack us. There he was, sitting in his car about two rows back from us. I yell at Marissa, "GO, GO, GO! He's here!" I took off running towards Kannon's dorm. I saw KC's car drive off behind Marissa. I kept running and running until I got to Kannon's dorm. *Please, please be understanding*, I thought to myself. I called Kannon's phone once I reached his dorm so I could ask him to come to the entrance and let me in. He answered the phone with the sound of sleep in his voice. I said to him, while trying to catch my breath, "I NEED HELP!"

CHAPTER 18

HELP

Kannon rushed to the dorm entrance door with a puzzled look on his face. He said to me, “What’s wrong, Dynver?” I placed my head on his chest and tried to bury it in his chest like I would normally do my favorite pillow back home. I cried while I repeatedly continued to say, “I need help, I need help”. We walked back to his room and my entire body was shaking right. He was holding me and rocking me while I cried and said to me, “Talk to me, tell me what’s wrong?” I stopped sobbing for a second to look into his concerned eyes. I stared up at him with my face all wet with tears and I said, “Please understand me.” Kannon looked back into my eyes and said to me, “Just tell me.”

Here goes nothing, I opened my mouth and started from the beginning.

Kannon held me close and asked me, “What now?” I told him I don’t know and that I’m worried Marissa may have not gotten away. I could feel Kannon’s heart thumping rapidly on my face. I told him I didn’t want to worry him with all of this. Kannon looked at me and said, "We have to go to the police and tell them everything. I know you don't want to, but we must if it will mean saving Marissa's life and maybe even your own." Kannon removed my arms from being wrapped around him and held my hands. He said to me, using a more demanding tone, "We're going to the police station. Now!" I pulled myself together and waited by the door as he pulled a shirt over his head. Yes, he was helping, and yes, he seemed concerned, but I still didn't know what he thought. If he thought I brought all of this on myself. I was just embarrassed to tell my story again, this time to the police. I was afraid of the questions they were going to ask, especially when I was the one who started it.

On the ride to the police station, I noticed we were near Marissa's hotel. I asked Kannon to pull over so that I could check and see if she made it back to the hotel yet. He said to me,
"Dynver, we don't have time for this, we need to get to the police station now." I screamed at him, "STOP THE CAR KANNON!". He stopped the car. I told him I needed to check before we go to the police station. My gut was telling me this was what I needed to do. Something inside of me knew Marissa needed my help right now, this very second. Kannon drove into the hotel parking lot and I saw her car, but I also saw KC's. I

looked at Kannon and I told him, “He has her.” Kannon looked at me and repeated, “Dynver, we need to go to the police station.” I didn’t want to leave her. I looked at Kannon as I was exiting the vehicle and told him, “You go to the police, I’m going to help her.” He responded back to me with a pleading voice, “Dynver, get back in the car, you can help her by going to the police. Dynver the police station is just down the road.” Kannon did not understand why it was important for me to stay here. I didn't move an inch after Kannon pleaded for me to get back in the car. I stood there in silence to see if I could hear Marissa scream. As if that would be my cue to save her. I didn't hear anything but the cars passing by. Kannon grabbed me by the hand and forced me in the car. I was stuck. Frozen. I don’t know what I was thinking I could do to help her without getting myself hurt. I wasn’t thinking and clearly neither was Kannon because all of sudden he said, “Dynver, I left my phone in my room, where’s your phone. We can call the police and they will be here in seconds.” Thank God for Kannon’s quick thinking because the thought of what KC could be doing to Marissa right now had me mentally gone away from earth. I called the police station and told them I had information about a sexual assault that was happening right now and gave the address of the hotel and the room number 715. I prayed they got to her quickly, before KC finished and left. Kannon and I sat in the car silently. I didn't feel like talking anyway. I was too busy trying to concentrate on the entrance door of the hotel and look for any signs of help for Marissa.

Two minutes felt like forever. Where were the police? I thought Kannon said it was just down the street. I should hear some sirens or something by now. I got impatient and I said to Kannon, "Screw this, I'm going in." Kannon jumped out of the car and tried to stop me. I forced myself away from Kannon and marched into the building. Kannon hesitated but then rushed behind me. We were on the elevator and I could tell Kannon was regretting every decision he was making right now. I told him he could just go wait outside for the cops. Kannon took a deep breath right before the elevator stopped and said to me ,"I will not let him hurt you again." We exited the elevator and began to walk towards Marissa's room. Everything was happening in slow motion right now. My heart and Kannon's heart were beating louder and louder. I just wished I could hear the police sirens right now to end all of this. We reached the room and stood at the door. I was shaking. I thought to myself, what if he had already killed her? I didn't want to see that. We listened at the door to see if we could hear any movement. I could hear noises, but I could not make out what they could be. I wanted to turn around now and wait on the cops like Kannon had suggested. That rescue girl that was in my spirit to do the right thing had suddenly turned into a frightened little girl who still didn't want to face her abuser. Kannon stood beside me, unsure of what he had gotten himself involved with. I thought to myself, *be brave, don't let KC get away with it. Embarrass him, let the world see what he has done to you and Marissa*. Feeling just a tad bit better I lifted my hand and knocked on the door. The room got quiet and I spoke to the door with fear in my voice, "KC, it's me, Dynver." He didn't respond, so I spoke to the door again, "KC, please let Marissa go, the police are already on their way". KC still didn't respond. Kannon looked at me and grabbed my hand and said to me, "Come on Dynver, you tried". KC opened the door with a gun in his hand and aimed it directly at Kannon. I screamed, "NO KC!" He responded with, "Calm down. Dynver baby, you asked for this, so you and your little friend here needs to come inside before things get ugly". Kannon and I walked slowly into the room. I thought to myself, *dammit Dynver you've done it again*. My senseless acts had now placed both my life and Kannon's in danger.

We entered the room and I could see Marissa tied to the bed by her hands and feet. He had her laying there naked with blood leaking from her nose and lip. I ran to her to let her know that I was there and the police were on the way. Once the door was closed, KC hit Kannon in the back of the head with his gun. I screamed, "Someone help! Someone please!" KC started laughing as he was tying Kannon's arms and legs together. I still didn't hear the police sirens. KC finished up tying Kannon then kicked him in the stomach. I screamed out, "Why KC? Why?" He looked at me and said, "I love you Dynver, and I love Marissa too. Just like I thought I loved all of them. I want us to be this one big happy family. Me, you, and Marissa. But you had to end what we had going on. I thought you were smart enough to know you couldn't just leave me and come to Florida and start an entire new life without me. I told you, you belong to me and I want you all to myself. Marissa understands, don't you babe?" I looked at Marissa who is barely conscious right now. She tried to move her head in agreement with KC because she was scared. I know she is. He continued, "Now this is the plan, we're going to sneak out of here silently before the cops get here and begin our new life together just me, you, and Marissa." I thought to myself he had won. There were no police sirens and no one apparently had heard my screams because no one had come to our rescue. My mind left my body as I stared at Kannon all tied up on the floor. I did this to him and in order for me to save him I would follow KC's every demand.

CHAPTER 19

THE PLAN

I looked to KC and said, "I told you I loved you first, do you remember? You didn't tell me back and then you avoided me for days until I found out about Marissa. I thought you loved me KC." I got off the bed and started walking towards him. He watched my every move, so I made sure not to move too fast. He still had the gun in his right hand, so I softly touched his left hand and slid his fingers between mine. I stared into his eyes knowing what my eyes were capable of, soul snatchers, and said, “All I needed you to say is that you loved me and I would’ve come back to you.” KC leaned in and kissed me on my lips. I made sure to kiss him back. “I’m ready KC, I’m ready to go before the cops get here.” KC placed the gun in the front of his pants under his shirt. We untied Marissa together. He untied her feet and I untied her hands. While I was helping Marissa put her clothes on, I finally heard them. The sirens were outside. I looked to KC and told him to hurry, we needed to move fast. KC glanced out of the window and said to me, “Change of plans Dynver, she will only slow us down. It’s only me and you who must go now.”

I looked at Marissa’s face and then down at Kannon’s. I told them both goodbye, feeling like I wasn’t going to ever see them again. KC and I exited the room and get on the elevator. We would be able to walk right out the door and pass the police because I didn’t give a description of KC and there were no markings on me to indicate I was in any type of trouble. I could just run towards the cops and cause a scene. Yes, that was what I would do. When the elevator door opened KC grabbed me by my arm and pulled me closer to him and pressed the gun against my back. “Don’t try nothing stupid”, KC said to me while squeezing my arm. Well there went that plan. We exited the elevator and right there in the lobby stood the police officer. He didn't even look my way as we walked right past him.

When we got to KC's car, he opened the door for me and shut it once I was settled in the car. Wow, what a perfect gentleman he suddenly had become. I watched KC closely as he walked in front of his car to enter the driver's side. I remembered telling the police the room number. When they got to the room and found Kannon and Marissa, I'm sure they would tell them what happened and be able to give a description of KC and his car so they could rescue me. My nerves were still out of whack. Just like normal, KC wasn't really saying much, and I needed him to start talking so I could see where his mind was. He clearly didn't trust me yet because he held the gun to my side when we exited the elevator. I had to gain his trust quickly. I slid my hand across to him and held his hand. I asked him, "So where are we going?" Without taking his eyes off the road he said, "I don't know yet". I thought to myself, damn neither of us have a plan. I said back to him, "It's ok, as long as we're together". Oh Lord, I hoped he was starting to trust me. He said back to me, "I know I hurt you in the past, Dynver, but you've got to understand, I didn't mean for any of this to happen. I never meant to hurt you, but I knew I needed to make you listen to me and do as I say so that we could be happy." I thought to myself, he meant so that HE could be happy. He didn't care about my happiness and never had. He just cared about what he wanted.

KC continued to talk while we were holding hands. I noticed the blue lights creeping up on us. Yes, they were coming to my rescue. KC finally quit talking and looked in his rearview and noticed them too. I told him, "Be calm KC, they're probably not looking for us". KC was unable to keep his cool and let go of my hand and placed both hands on the wheel and began to drive faster and faster. I screamed, "KC, just stop! Just stop, you're scaring me." He didn't stop. I wanted to grab the wheel and just take control, but I was too afraid. The police were getting closer and closer. KC had them on a high speed chase.

I was sitting there holding the seatbelt across my chest. I felt like this was the end. If KC didn't stop this car, he was going to lose control of the car and we would flip a thousand times and then that would be the end. I begged him and begged him to stop, or slow down at least but he did not listen. We were near the beach. The same beach I went to when I first arrived in Florida. The same beach Kannon and I had our first kiss at. I thought to myself, if I could only be sitting on the beach right now.

My favorite place in the world. I could hear the ocean waves rushing towards me and imagine them washing the sand off my feet. I just wanted to feel free.

I looked back and saw all the red and blue lights blinking and I heard the sirens echoing in my ear. I looked over at KC driving so fiercely and I placed my hand on his thigh. I looked him in his eyes so angelically and I pleaded with him one more time, this time using only one word and letting my eyes do the rest. I said to him, “Stop”, and KC looked back at me and the car began to decelerate. KC stopped the car and I was relieved. We sat there while the police gave orders and waited for us to exit the vehicle. I sat there with my face in my hands and took long breaths in and out. I didn’t have the energy to move. KC was not saying much and for the first time I was glad he had nothing to say. The officer gave the order again for KC and I to exit the car with our hands up and lay down on the ground. KC looked at me and asked, “Are you ready?” I nodded my head yes and we got ready to exit the car. We were standing outside of the car and the officer was yelling for us to lay down and before I could lay my body on the ground, KC pulled out his gun and began shooting at the cops. I started running towards the cops on the opposite side of the car. Bullets were flying all over my head. I didn’t know if it was KC's bullets or the cops aiming at me for running. I fell right in front of one officer and as he was helping me get out of the way I looked back to see that KC had been shot.

I was sitting in the back of the police car and I prayed and cried the entire ride to the hospital. I didn't know if KC was dead and I didn't care right now. I didn't know where Marissa and Kannon were, but I was thankful they were able to send help my way. We arrived at the hospital and the nurses checked me out. I told them that I'm ok and just wanted to know where Kannon and Marissa were so they could know that I'm alright. The nurse told me that I will have to speak to the detectives first and then they would give me information on Kannon and Marissa. I waited patiently on the detectives to arrive.

I spoke with the detectives letting them know everything from the beginning to the end, all over again. They took all the notes on their little notepad and told me KC was still alive, but he was in critical condition. If he lived, we would have to go to trial. They asked me, "Do you think you could handle a trial?" I looked them in their eyes and said, "I'm not embarrassed anymore, I will be ready". The detective looked at me and said, “OK”. I asked her about Kannon and Marissa, she told me they were both here and when I was ready I could go see them.

I walked down the hall and the first room I got to was Marissa’s. She was sitting up in the bed with bandages around her arm and face. KC had broken her arm and her nose before Kannon and I arrived. I walked into her room and said, “Hey, thank you for helping save me.” Marissa, unable to smile with her lip swollen and sore, smiled at me with her eyes. I updated her on the information the detectives provided me with about KC and she looked like she wished they would have killed him. I gave her the same look back. I knew she couldn’t do much talking because it hurt for her to move her mouth so I let her know that when she was healed and all better that we could talk then. I walked over to Marissa and gave her a kiss on her forehead. I knew we didn’t know each other that well but after this event we shared a lot in common and I knew I could definitely use a kiss on the forehead right now.

I entered Kannon’s room and he was sitting on the edge of the bed with his head in his hands. I walked towards him and I grabbed his hands for him to look up at me. Kannon looked up at me and pulled me into his arms and just held me. I told Kannon I was sorry for getting him involved and for making such foolish decisions. I began to ramble off what I should've, would've or could've done and Kannon stopped me and said, "It's ok Dynver, we live and we learn. I'm just glad no one had to die today." I told Kannon that he was right and from this day forward I would make better decisions. Kannon's parents arrived and they were hovering all over him, checking out his bruises while kissing him on his forehead. I slipped out of the room before they found out exactly who I was and that I was the reason why this happened to their son. Seeing how his parents were all over him, I felt that it was time I called my own family and finally tell my mom everything. I guess it was true what my mom always said, 'What's done in the dark will always come to light.'

CHAPTER 20

THE TRIAL

I met up with my lawyer to prepare for the trial. I had not seen KC in months now. It would be scary to see him in court, but I was ready to face him. I was sure they were going to give him life without parole. During their investigations they had discovered that KC had dated two other girls, who were reported missing. I wondered if he killed them or if they just changed their entire identity to get away from him. I thought that could have been the other girls' belongings that Marissa found in KC's room. KC had already gotten rid of that box before Marissa could get a chance to tell the cops where it was. Here he was already making us look like little liars and the trial hadn't even begun yet.

Kannon and I remained just friends afterwards. Not friends, like we were before. Just hey and bye type of friends. We didn't hangout and we didn't talk over the phone, we just had small talk in person when passing by. I didn't think he could ever look at me the same after all of this. His suspension was lifted due to KC planting the drugs in his locker, as I suspected he had. I still didn't understand KC's plan of why he wanted to ruin Kannon. Why did he have to enter my life through Amber? What was his reason for any of this? I guess we would never know unless KC decided to start talking. Yeah right, talking was something he was just not going to do.

I spoke with Marissa just days before the trial began. She looked better and was doing well. She told me she was going to therapy for the traumatizing experience and suggested that I do the same. I agreed with her, but I had a hard enough time finally opening up to my mom and everyone else. I didn't believe continually talking about it would do me any justice. I just wanted to move on and forget any of this had ever happened. The meet up with Marissa was very brief. We were not supposed to be discussing the trial and it was not like we had anything else in common to discuss. Before Marissa and I parted ways, she said to me, "Dynver, please promise that you will try therapy. You may not think you need it now but in order for you to move on with your life and have healthy new relationships, you're going to need it then." She gave me a hug and the same kiss on the forehead I had given to her when she was in the hospital.

The trial began and one by one testimonials of KC's actions were displayed right in front of him. He sat there in the courtroom without any emotion on his face. He sat there, stone faced, no flicker of evilness or sadness. I tried not to look at him, advised by my lawyer, but I couldn't help myself. I wanted to stare into his eyes and search for the answers of why. KC eyes finally connected with mine. I searched for some sort of answer or emotion and there was nothing there. Why was he so empty? Had I done this to him? I felt like I was the reason he was here right now. Why was I such a problem creator? I ruined his life, I ruined Marissa's life, I almost ruined Kannon's life. I broke down on the stand, the tears were pouring down my face. I screamed out for everyone to hear me in the courtroom, "I'M SORRY, I'M SO SORRY, THIS IS ALL MY FAULT, I DID THIS TO EVERYONE!" I looked into KC's eyes and said, "Please forgive me, please forgive me". They asked me to leave the stand and I didn't move. I sat there watching all the eyes in the courtroom staring back at me with confusion written all over their faces. I watched my mom and Kimber sit in the courtroom hurting for me and I knew I caused their pain. When I looked into Marissa's and Kannon's eyes, I felt like I had let them down. I thought I was ready to face KC and embarrass him for all his wrong doings. Instead I was embarrassed again. The deputy approached me and assisted me with exiting the stand. The deputy escorted me out to the hallway and my mom and Kimber followed.

I stood there in my mom's arms and I just cried, and cried, and cried. Kimber rubbed my back to comfort me, but nothing was working. I just wanted to get out of there. I just wanted to go home. Marissa was right, I needed therapy. I knew what KC did was wrong, but I believed I had caused all of it. After I calmed down enough, I was able to enter the courtroom again to wait on the verdict. The Judge said, "Mr. Kelvin Crowe will you please stand." I thought to myself, I never even knew his real name. Why did this even matter to me? The Judge continued, "On the charges against Mr. Crowe has the Jury reached a verdict?" Oh God, I was nervous. The jury had reached a verdict. They found KC guilty of all charges against him. I dropped my head into my hands. Marissa and her family cried tears of joy. Kannon and his family were pleased with the verdict. My mom and Kimber were happy all of this was over. Why did I still feel bad?

My mom took me and Kimber on a vacation afterwards so that I could get away and feel free again. She knew how much I loved the beach, she felt this would be perfect for me. The Judge sentenced KC to

10 years in prison and while he's there he's ordered to attend mental health sessions as well. I stood there on the beach thinking to myself. Everyone was getting the help they needed except for me. I decided I would take Marissa's advice and see a therapist and maybe the therapist could explain to me why I felt the way I do. Why did I feel like everything was my fault and that I could have controlled all of this? Why did I feel like I should be punished as well?

Before we returned from vacation my mom scheduled a therapy appointment for me with Dr. Chandler. He was the same therapist my mom used for her grief. I walked into his office unsure of how I felt or what I should feel. Dr. Chandler greeted me with his perfect smile, firm handshake, and charming eyes. He asked me to sit on the couch and make myself comfortable. I sat on the couch staring at this handsome man. I think he was about 35, maybe 37 years old. Maybe I should date much older than 3 to 5 years of age. Oh God, I had a problem. Why was I immediately crushing on my therapist? I thought to myself, *please help me Dr. Chandler, please help me*. Dr. Chandler sat in his chair with his notepad and pencil and asked, "Ms. Dynver, where should we begin?" and I responded with, "It all started with a simple crush."

Made in the USA
Columbia, SC
23 April 2022

59365822R00071